What They Don't Tell You About Getting Remarried

By J.K. Weyant

This is a work of fiction. Names, characters, organizations, events, and incidents are either products of the author's imagination or are used fictitiously (mostly.)

Dedication

To the divorcees who are willing to risk your heart again for the one you always should have been with.

To my husband, Dan, the one who I gave my heart to and will never fear that you'll break it.

Table of contents

Prologue

I was stupid. I was so, so stupid for doing this.

But I had to be sure. What if I found out today that he was? What would I do?

I caught up to Luke in his black truck but stayed far behind so he wouldn't see me. I prayed to God his cop instincts wouldn't alert him that he was being followed.

I watched him turn the corner and pull behind the restaurant called Bleu's that sat between Swan's Jewelry and the liquor store. I frowned.

Why would he park behind the building and not in front?

I quickly parked a distance away, then jumped out of the car and crossed the street. A horn honked as I hurried, but I ignored it and ran to the corner of the strip mall to hide before Luke saw me. I peeked around the corner and saw him on his phone, talking to someone and looking toward the buildings. Just then the door to Swan's Jewelry opened and out walked a woman, who was also on her phone. She looked around and when she saw

Luke, she smiled and waved. He returned the gesture as she put up one finger for him to wait then disappeared back inside.

Dread filled me as I stared at the door. My gaze flitted to Luke who was still sitting in his truck waiting.

Waiting for a beautiful red-haired woman in the black dress.

It was confirmed…Luke was cheating on me.

Chapter One

See, Progress

"Luke Price!" I scolded him as I walked into his kitchen. He was standing by the island, in sweatpants without a shirt, about to take the first sip of his coffee. His brown eyes looked at me sleepily and a five o'clock shadow darkened his cheeks.

"Where is my makeup bag? It was sitting on the counter in the bathroom."

He lowered the mug slowly and gave me a look that reminded me I was only wearing one of his white t-shirts that barely covered the tops of my thighs.

"I put it in the closet," he finally answered after giving me a heated once-over.

My ears grew warm, and my toes curled involuntarily as I walked closer to him.

We had become inseparable the last few months and just like a new couple, we had barely come up for air.

Who needed oxygen anyhow when you had Luke Price for air?

He pulled me by the hem of the t-shirt until I was pressed tightly against him.

"My bag goes home with me; it doesn't stay here," I said breathlessly, trying not to lose focus as to why I was scolding him.

He lowered his lips in that tantalizing smile that made me know where his thoughts were.

"This is a home," he added, brushing his lips against mine, making me struggle to think.

"Not *my* home."

This had been our disagreement over the last few weeks. I wouldn't leave my things at his house even though he'd left a few things at mine. Putting my bag in the closet was his way of trying to get me to stay over more than just two nights. He knew how I felt about being with someone again and instead of forcing me, he slowly, nonchalantly started encouraging me. Though, nonchalant wasn't his thing.

He sighed and pulled back from the kiss in annoyance. "It's just a small bag, Brynn. It's not a whole dresser drawer."

I pressed my lips together feeling bad. I was being ridiculous, and I knew it. It was my scared, divorced ass that was the problem, not him. He was perfect, too perfect.

"I know," I murmured. "Just give me time."

He looked skyward and sighed again and that gave me the perfect opportunity to kiss his long, tan, muscular neck.

His hands tightened on my hips and in a second, he lifted me up onto the island as his kisses grew more feverish.

"Don't knock the coffee over!" I mewled between kisses.

But we were too far gone to care.

Ugh, that honeymoon stage of dating. It was delicious. Intoxicating. And it made everything in me melt like a high school girl the minute I locked eyes with him.

Unfortunately, we had jobs and we had to go to them. He kissed me before he went to his squad car and got in. I waved from the porch steps, a coffee cup in my hands, as he drove out of the driveway.

Luke Price had been the best guy I could've found after my divorce. It had been a rough year of trying to find myself while maintaining some of my sanity. Luke had chiseled away at my cold heart and gave me the courage to try again. To try dating and being with someone even though I was scared out of my mind.

My family loved him, including my dad and overprotective brothers who played poker with him at the fire department on Friday nights. They'd treated him like another brother. Part of me loved that and the other part was freaked out.

We hadn't said those three scary words: *I love you*, but neither of us were rushing it.

I went back upstairs to get my makeup bag out of the closet where Luke had made room for it on an empty shelf. I swallowed hard at the sight. It was subtle, but I knew what he was doing. He wasn't forcing me to commit but letting it be on my terms…in a way.

From my overnight bag, I pulled out a cute blouse and skirt and got dressed quickly. I went downstairs, turning the lights off as I went, and saw a thermos on the counter. A pink one with a note written in his masculine handwriting.

This is from my house. Make sure you bring it back.

Yeah, because he loves the color pink.

I picked it up and opened the top to peer down into the dark abyss of coffee.

I'd been with Luke for three months and though we had rushed things in the bedroom, we were taking the rest of our relationship extra slow, mainly because of me. I was gun shy, and making sure I didn't get my heart broken again. And honestly, Luke was definitely the type to break a few hearts. He was patient with me even though I freaked out at leaving something at his house. It was almost scary how easily we'd slipped into a routine together and how domesticated we'd become after only three months.

It was nice having someone to talk to, go home to, and someone who actually wanted to spend time with me.

I locked the house from the inside since I'd refused to take a key. I got in my car, took a drink from the pink thermos, and drove to work.

When I arrived at Feather Blue, Emma was waiting for me.

It had been several months since we found the previous owner's missing diamonds in the old cash register. When we tried to give them back to the Emerson family, they insisted we keep them since we'd been through an ordeal before finding them. We sold the diamonds and split the profit. Emma was using her portion for her wedding and honeymoon, but I hadn't figured out what to do with mine yet. It was sitting in a bank collecting some interest.

Business at Feather Blue had really picked up after the news got out that we found the missing diamonds. We were so busy that Emma decided to build an addition to the store and hire two more employees. This would also allow Emma to have the time off she needed to plan the wedding. She asked both Mackayla and me to be in the wedding, but she'd given me a role that was very humbling, maid of honor.

I'd been in several weddings for friends, my sisters-in-law, and of course my own, and knew I wanted to make Emma's wedding special.

She held a coffee cup in her hands and a knowing smile on her face as we walked into the store.

"That cup doesn't look familiar," she said as we shut and locked the back door behind us.

"Luke got it for me."

She eyed me over her shoulder with a smirk. "Spent the night over there last night?"

My thoughts went to this morning's quickie on the island and my face heated for a moment. "Yes, you're down to nineteen more questions then you're done for the year," I half joked.

She chuckled. "All I'm saying is that it's clear you're both obsessed with each other and you, trying to act like you are not, isn't working."

We put our lunches in the small fridge and sat down at desks we'd arranged in the back.

"I like him a lot. He knows that. The world knows that and I'm fine with it."

She turned on her computer then twisted in the seat to give me a motherly look, the diamond on her finger flashing. "Brynn, you won't even keep your freaking toothbrush there or a pair of shoes or even a thread from a sweater. That's showing some commitment issues for sure."

I turned on my computer and the background flashed to a Caribbean scene.

"I'm getting there, Em, slowly. It's taken me a lot to get to this point and he's being patient."

She clicked her tongue. "I love you, Brynn, you know I do, but he's not the 'roll around in the sheets until he's gray' kind of guy. He's a committed man that wants a life with a wife."

"Has he said anything to Sam?"

"No."

Her answer was too quick, and I narrowed my gaze. Emma had always been an awful liar. It's why she made a good best friend.

"Emma Argo, you better tell me the truth. Did Luke say something?"

She tried to avoid eye contact, but it didn't work. She finally sighed. "Kind of, well not really. Sam swore me to secrecy!"

"Spill."

"When Sam asked him how it was going, Luke said it was going 'good.'"

I reminded myself to never give her any information because if she was tortured for it, she would sing like a canary. "That doesn't exactly sound bad."

"No, it just sounds *good.*"

I stared at her. It had only been three months, what other word was he supposed to use?

"Anything else?" I asked, prodding.

Her lips thinned. "Well, when Sam told him we were moving in together, Sam asked him if that would happen for you guys and Luke just kind of shook his head and said, 'not until she's ready.'"

I could almost hear Luke saying that because I'd heard it many times. He had given me the reins to take the lead in our relationship so I didn't get spooked, but how much was he giving up?

"Okay," I responded dumbly.

"Brynn, don't look like that!" Emma argued, seeming guilty. "All I'm trying to say is give the guy a little hope. Leave some stuff at his house. Relationships are two ways. If it's only one, it won't work."

I listened to her words. She was right. I had to give a little, it was Luke after all.

"You've been reading those marriage books again, haven't you?"

Her face flamed and she turned back to her computer. "I don't know what you're talking about."

I stared at my toothbrush and my makeup bag sitting on the counter.

"You can do this," I whispered to myself. "Just leave it here."

I itched to put them in my overnight duffle but instead I set the makeup bag on the shelf and added my toothbrush to the holder by the sink.

See, that wasn't so hard.

Luke walked into the bathroom shirtless, grinned at me and gave me a kiss before smacking my butt and stripping.

He glanced over to the sink and saw my toothbrush in the holder next to his own. I saw something in him change in that moment, an emotion filtered through him, but he didn't look at me. He climbed into the shower and turned it on.

"What's the plans for the weekend, Sweetheart?" he asked through the steam of the shower.

I brushed out my hair as I answered him. "My parents on Sunday for dinner." It felt so natural, and it took me by surprise that I didn't retreat at how couply we were.

See, progress.

Emma would be proud.

"Maybe some fishing?" I suggested.

He chuckled. "Got you addicted now."

I turned my head sideways to look into the shower and bit my lip.

Definitely addicted.

Chapter Two

Selling Out

Sunday dinners with my family were something I didn't get to go to a lot when Owen and I were married. He hated going and hated Cold Spring.

The first time Luke joined us, it was slightly awkward. Well, only for me. Luke fit in like he'd been born one of my brothers.

Ick. Remind me never to think that again.

But it was easy for him to sit and chat with everyone. Even my niece and nephew loved him.

When we pulled into my parents' driveway with pasta salad in my lap, Luke leaned over to kiss me before we got out of the truck.

It was a good kiss.

"What was that for?"

His lips curled up and he kept his hand on my chin as he looked into my eyes.

"Can't I have any excuse to kiss my girlfriend?"

Girlfriend. It sounded so juvenile. Like it didn't quite work for us since we were twenty-nine and thirty-three, and it had taken a little while to get used to it. His eyes were filled with that emotion...the three-letter phrase that made me feel all sorts of ways. And also scared the shit out of me.

"No," I answered back dumbly.

As if he knew where my scaredy-cat thoughts were, he sighed and got out of the truck. I swallowed hard, thinking of my conversation with Emma. Luke never wanted to have a fling with someone; he was more of a commitment man. If I didn't commit, he'd find someone who would.

I got out of the truck and Luke met me halfway around to join me as we walked up to the front door. The family was already there, and the kids ran to the door to greet us.

"Luke! Luke!" Aaron yelled and Luke gladly lifted him into his arms.

"Hey bud, how did you do at your last soccer game?"

I smiled at the sight. Dad's face lit up the moment he saw Luke and then Dylan and Mark came to corral Luke away to the living room. He threw me a smile before following them and I walked into the kitchen. My sisters-in-law were helping my mother finish up the last bit of dinner.

"Brynn!" Kate said, hugging me tightly. Dylan's wife Lauren waved as she kept her hands around a glass of water. My mother, always happy to see her daughter, quickly kissed me before going back to stirring whatever was in a large pot on the stove.

"Where's your hunk of a man?" Lauren asked.

I put the pasta salad down with an eye roll. "With the men. They take him immediately as we come in the door for whatever reason."

"They are obsessed with him," Kate whispered. "Mark invites him over to their poker table every Friday. They even ask Sam to sit with them."

That was a surprise. Sam was engaged to Emma. Back in high school, Mark and Emma were in a committed relationship until Mark broke her heart and left for college where he met Kate. But that was years ago. They all lived in the same town now and things had changed.

"That's good," I said quietly to her.

She pulled me aside while Lauren and Mom talked about something next weekend.

"Do you think Emma would mind if I stopped into the store? I just…I just want things to be better and not so awkward."

I pressed my lips together, wishing I could tell her yes. I wasn't sure how Emma felt about it now. She was only eight months out from marrying Sam and was happier than ever, but did that mean she over what happened with Mark? I wasn't sure.

"Let me talk to her and I'll let you know," I said back, squeezing Kate's hand.

She nodded as we walked back into the kitchen and began to set the table for dinner.

"Brynn, why don't you go get the kids and boys?" Mom suggested.

I walked to the living room where the men were watching the game, each with a beer in his hand. Luke was sitting on the floor leaning up against the couch, legs outstretched and beside him sat Aaron, playing with his GI Joe toy. My heart stopped at the sight.

He was a perfect match for my family. They never liked Owen, more like hated him, but Luke...he was one of them. He was so easy going and everyone flocked to be around him.

Why couldn't I change for him?

"Aunt Brynnie, are you okay?" Bailey asked, sitting on my father's lap as she looked up at me.

I sniffed and straightened as all the men's eyes focused on me, including Luke's.

"Dinner is ready," I finally said.

Everyone got up and left but Luke waited until I was by him to pull me against his side.

"You alright, Clark? You look a little starry eyed."

"I'm fine."

Too fine. So fine I want to take you to my old bedroom and make some better memories.

We all sat down at the table and within a few minutes, conversations were going and everyone was in good spirits.

"How is business at Feather Blue?" Mom asked.

"Good! It's really picked up since we found the diamonds," I said, taking a bite of salad.

Luke's leg touched mine and just that little bit of contact made me remember he was there. Not like I could forget.

"What are you going to do with all the money, Aunt Brynnie?" Bailey asked.

People had been asking me that a lot and I still wasn't sure. "Maybe your college," I joked.

She didn't like that because she hated school. Mark who was sitting next to Aaron said, "I don't have to bother worrying about college for Aaron. He's definitely not going."

As Mark said that, Aaron pulled a partial green bean out of his nose then giggled.

"Have you stopped any bad guys this week, Mr. Luke?" Bailey asked, intrigued by him.

He chuckled. "No, not this week. Lucky for us, Cold Spring is very safe except for a few robbers here and there." He glanced over at me, knowing where his and my thoughts were. It was on the robbery that had almost injured Emma.

"I'm sure it's different from working for the NYPD," Dylan commented.

That made me think of the raid that had killed one of Luke's friends in the police force and the tattoo on his chest. A tattoo of the coordinates of where his friend had fallen. A tattoo I was very familiar with since I'd touched and kissed that chest many times.

I cleared my throat and took a sip of water to distract my heated thoughts.

"Yeah," Luke replied. "It's a lot different. I don't regret the move though." He glanced towards me again and I felt his hand on my thigh. "Best move I've made in a while."

Of course, I felt a blush stain my cheeks at his words because he wasn't just talking about the job. He was talking about us.

I slid a little closer to him and looked down at his hand resting gently on my leg. It was possessive but sweet and made me feel all sorts of ways.

After dinner was over, we said our goodbyes–the boys planning a fishing trip to the Finger Lakes in the spring—and left to go to my place. I had made sure to switch the sheets and clean up before Luke stayed over. I'd found out early on he was a sort of neat freak. He liked things a certain way and I partially blamed that on the police academy.

When we made it back to my house, Felix was waiting patiently on the counter for our arrival. The cat was obsessed with Luke which was funny considering he wasn't much of a cat person, or so he claimed, but he made sure to give ample enough attention to the black cat.

I dropped my stuff in the kitchen and started to take my earrings out as Luke petted Felix.

"I think I want to get a dog," I said casually.

He looked up at me and seemed surprised. “Really?”

“I think if I ask my landlord he would let me. Do you like dogs?” I thought of his interaction with Barney, his dad’s dog, but remembered he wouldn’t let him in his house.

He shrugged. “Yes, I do. I’ve just never had one of my own.”

I checked my phone and saw that Emma had sent me at least six pictures of different color schemes and centerpiece ideas.

“What’s up?” Luke asked, coming up behind to wrap his arms around my waist.

“Emma,” I said with a chuckle. “She’s so excited about this wedding. I think she already has her dress picked out.”

Luke smiled softly and looked over my shoulder. There was a bright red dress with a long slit in it and Luke made a happy growl. “You’d look nice in that.”

I scoffed. “I doubt we’ll be wearing anything like that.”

“Sam said we’re wearing black suits, but I haven’t heard anything else yet.”

Sam had asked Luke to be in the wedding, however, it wasn’t a grand gesture like a beautiful necklace that Emma had given me. It was more like a grunt from Sam and a grunt back from Luke and that had sealed the deal on being a groomsman.

Men.

I had planned my first wedding out down to miniscule details like the centerpiece arrangement having three candles instead of four or our bouquets having the exact amount of each flower. I had been obnoxious. Owen's mother had put the pressure on me by listing everyone I had to invite and what was expected of a Rally wedding. We had it at a country club with two hundred people in attendance and an expensive dinner. It had all been to show off their wealth and had nothing to do with Owen and me actually getting married.

Not again. And who knew if I would even get remarried again.

"We'll figure it out," I said belatedly. He kissed my temple and moved his hands onto my hips.

"Have I told you how beautiful you are?" His question, well statement, made my heart beat a little harder as his lips moved to my neck and placed small light kisses there.

I shivered. "Yes, but I like hearing it."

The following day at Feather Blue, Emma and I worked together behind the counter as our part-timers helped customers in the dressing rooms.

I thought about Kate's question that she asked during dinner at my parents on Sunday. Now might be a good time to broach that subject with Emma.

"Em, so um, Kate wanted to stop in the store sometime soon. Would that be okay?"

Emma seemed a little caught off guard and looked at me. "She does?"

I nodded.

I was trying to gauge what Emma was thinking but it was difficult. She answered a question from one of the part-timers then looked down at the reports in her front of her. It would upset Kate if she said no but she'd understand if she did. It'd been a long time since Mark, and they'd both moved on.

"Um, sure, I guess," she mumbled.

I didn't see that as a go so I made a mental note to text Kate and say not yet. I didn't want to push Emma.

"I think I'm putting my house up on the market soon," Emma said, changing the subject.

"Really?" I asked, intrigued. "You'll be moving into Sam's?"

"It makes the most sense. He has a bigger house and more land. I'm thinking we can get a good price for my house, too."

I hadn't thought of buying a house recently…but Emma's was a nice size. With the money from the diamond…I would have a good down payment on it.

"When do you think you'll put it on the market?" I asked.

"Probably a few months, I want to make sure there's time to sell it before the wedding."

My lease with Frank would be up by the end of summer…it would be a good opportunity.

"Would you sell it to me?"

She looked shocked and stared at me for a few moments. "Are you serious?"

"I'd have to check into getting a mortgage, but I've been wanting to buy a house for a while now. I have the money for a downpayment."

She frowned, her blonde eyebrows meeting together. "What about Luke?"

I mimicked her frown. "What about Luke?"

"Haven't you talked about moving in together? Even if you decide to move in in like a year or two, you'd have to resell."

Move in…with Luke? With a man? I'd just started living on my own…I wasn't ready to even think about that.

So instead, I lied. "We aren't moving in together anytime soon. It hasn't even been a conversation between us."

"That's because you're scared of any word that revolves around commitment," she countered.

I stiffened. "Yes, kind of. You know that whole divorce thing? That will do it to you."

She sighed. “I know, Brynn. I just don’t want you to rush into this and regret it, especially if you and Luke get more serious.”

I couldn’t even lie and say we weren't serious because we were, but we’d only been dating for a few months, it wasn’t long enough to commit to living together.

“It’ll be fine, he knows how much I want to buy a house.”

She didn’t look convinced.

That weekend, I spent Friday night at Luke’s, and we sat cuddled on the couch watching a movie when I brought it up.

“Emma is selling her house. They decided they are going to move into Sam’s before they get married.”

Luke took a swig of his beer, still watching the TV. “That’s good.”

He wasn’t completely paying attention. “I was thinking I’d put an offer in when it goes on the market.”

His head snapped to me. *Well, that got his attention.*

“What?”

I shifted so I could face him completely. “Yeah, I have that money from the diamonds, so it’d work great as a downpayment for Emma’s house. It’s been a dream of mine to buy my own place. I never got to that point since my rent in New Rochelle was ridiculous."

He watched me, his eyes not showing much emotion and I wondered if I had upset him. "Is that what you want?"

"Yes."

But was it? What if Luke and I moved in together after a year? Would that be so bad? My anxiety boosted after I thought of how easily Owen had taken me off the lease and kicked me out. I had nowhere to go but home. I couldn't let that happen again. If I moved into Luke's house, it was *his* house, not my own. If he broke up with me, he could easily kick me out and I'd be back at square one: Mom and Dad's house. That had been humiliating enough.

He was quiet for a moment then turned back to the TV. "Okay."

It didn't sound convincing. "Just okay?"

He sighed. "What do you want me to say, Brynn?" He turned back and I saw irritation in his gaze.

I leaned away from him. "I don't know, maybe 'that's great, Sweetheart!'" I said in a deep voice, mimicking him. "Or 'if that's what you want, I support you.'"

He just stared at me. "Do you not want to live here one day?"

I swallowed at his words. He'd phrased them a certain way to not spook me but they still did.

"This is your house, Luke. Not mine. All of these things," I pointed around the room, "are yours."

He frowned. "Isn't that why you move your things in and mix it with mine so it's *ours*?"

"But the house will always be yours, it will never truly be mine." There was that anxiety again, the fear of being left with nothing.

"Fine, Brynn." He sat back on the couch and turned his attention to the TV again. I knew he was irritated.

Great.

The next day we didn't talk a lot but went on a double date with Emma and Sam. There was tension between us and immediately upon sitting down at a booth in Sullivan's, Emma noticed it.

She raised a brow at me, and I shook my head, not wanting to talk about it. We got beer and appetizers, and we talked mainly about the wedding. Emma sat across from me as I felt Luke's arm going around my shoulders. It was a truce. I leaned in to accept it. I didn't like fighting with him.

"The owners of Trinket Motors reported someone has been stealing catalytic converters off their cars. They think they're coming in from out of town," Sam said to Luke.

"Are you really discussing work?" Emma mused, holding Sam's hand.

He chuckled, looking at her beside him. "It's better than talking about wedding stuff."

She rolled her eyes. "Anyhow," she started with me. "I want to go bridesmaid shopping next week. I'm thinking we'll go to Tailor for You in the city and see if they have what we want."

"As long as the owner lets me off, I think I can go," I said in jest.

"Oh, stop it, you're an owner too!"

Emma had made me a partner after we'd worked together to put in the addition. It was still her pride and joy, but it felt good having some ownership in the clothing store. Being in retail was completely different than being a paralegal and I loved the change. I didn't miss having a sexist pig for a boss. My photography business was also doing well, and I picked up a lot during the summer and fall.

"We've had a few people stop in to ask about the diamonds. I had to tell them they aren't in the building anymore."

She laughed. "Can you imagine if we'd put it on display? We'd have break ins every day!"

"Do you think it'll all pay for the wedding?" I asked.

"I'm almost through all the money," Emma said with a wince. "This wedding isn't cheap."

Sam shook his head, looking annoyed by that, but not by her. "Are you definitely buying my house? My realtor said she's going to list it in the next few weeks. I told her you were interested."

Luke stiffened visibly beside me.

"Yes, I think I am. I'm going to go to the bank this week to talk about getting a loan," I said, ignoring Luke's reaction.

"You shouldn't rush it," Luke mumbled.

I glanced over at him. "Thought you said it was up to me?"

His jaw clenched with irritation. "I thought we'd have more time to discuss it."

"I don't need to discuss it. It's my decision."

I could feel the tension getting thicker and Sam and Emma looked equally as uncomfortable.

"I can always delay it," Emma suggested.

At the same time Luke and I both answered with opposite words.

Me: "No."

Luke: "Yes."

I narrowed my eyes on him, and he glared back.

"Oh look, the food!" Emma said with relief as it got to our table. The waitress didn't stay long enough but Luke removed his arm from around me and we started eating dinner. Luckily, Emma went onto a different subject but the tension between Luke and I grew.

Chapter Three

Those Three Words

It wasn't until we were headed back to Luke's house in silence that I finally said something.

"Listen, you knew I was serious about buying Emma's house. I thought we were over this."

"No, we weren't *over* this," he said with an angry tilt to his words that shocked me. "I know it's been a few years since I've been in a relationship but last time I checked, you discuss important things like this before jumping into anything."

I felt my anger flare. "We've been together for a few months, Luke! That doesn't qualify to get your permission on anything I do."

His jaw was clenched so tightly I thought it would crack. "I've never said anything about *permission*. It's called a discussion! Not sure what your idiot ex-husband did for situations like this, but we aren't repeating it."

With a low, angry yet calm voice, I said, "I want to have my own house, Luke."

"Why?" He glanced over while driving. We were almost home, well, to *his* home.

"Because I need it to be mine."

He knew there was more I wasn't going to talk about, and he ran a hand through his hair. "What did I tell you in the beginning, Brynn? You have to talk to me. What is it you want? You want your name to be added on the deed? Your name written on the side of the house? Because I'll do it if it makes you feel comfortable."

I didn't want to like him at that moment but his commitment to us and to working with me made my heart warm.

"I don't know," I finally said as we pulled into the driveway.

I stared out at the adorable home with the Hudson river behind it. It was beautiful. It was a dream home for any woman. I was stupid for not wanting to live here with Luke.

"Brynn," Luke said, getting my attention. "I don't want to control you. I just want to have a normal discussion when things are affecting both of us. Eventually, I want you to move in with me. This house is big enough for a family if we ever want to get to that point."

Oof, there goes that fear again.

"I know."

I was holding back from him, from the life we could have. Just like I'd tried months ago before I realized I wanted Luke. If I bought a house, it would be something I couldn't just drop and let go. It was a commitment too. And a big one.

"Promise me you'll think about it a little longer, don't make any decisions just yet?"

I saw hope in his eyes, so I agreed.

We went inside his house, and I changed into comfortable clothing. We went to bed together and I laid there with my hand spread across his bare chest.

I cared about Luke a lot. I wanted this to work between us, but I was still scared. It had nothing to do with him and everything to do with me. His lips brushed my forehead, and I titled my head up, so he could place a soft, sweet kiss on my lips.

"I want this to work, Luke," I whispered.

"I know you do, sweetheart. I'm not like your ex."

He wasn't. He was the exact opposite of him. It wasn't fair to make him suffer for it.

"I know."

His eyes were serious as he gazed into mine, his hand stroking my chin. "I love you, Brynn and I'm willing to fight for you."

My heart leaped out of my chest as I heard those words from his lips. For a moment I thought perhaps I'd hallucinated it but no, I didn't. He'd actually said the three words I was so scared of hearing and scared of saying back.

"Th-that's good," I said dumbly.

I saw the shift from his expression, and I put my head back down on his chest, not wanting to see it.

Shit. Had I really just said "that's good?" And even stuttered it?

I closed my eyes tightly as he sighed.

I could just say it, screw my fears and say it. I opened my mouth, but nothing came out, not even a squeak.

I tried again but still I was silent, as if my vocal cords had been cut out.

Did I just screw it up? Did I screw up what was happening between us because I was scared of saying I love you back?

The next morning, I felt awkward and depressed from the entire day before and especially when he'd said those three words that meant a whole lot. I'd stayed in bed instead of getting up when he did, and he came up to kiss my cheek as I pretended to sleep. When I heard the door shut, I finally crawled out of bed.

When I got to work, Emma saw me and looked away quickly. I sat down beside her at my desk and turned to her fully.

"I'm sorry about last night. Luke and I were having a disagreement."

She finally looked at me. "I'm sorry, I shouldn't have brought up the house thing in front of him."

"It's fine. We worked it out." Kind of. "I just feel bad we put you guys in that situation."

She waved her hand. "Sam and I have had our fair share of fights, so I get it."

"He said the three words to me last night after we made up." It came out like word vomit, and it made me green.

"What?" Her chair squeaked as she swiveled to stare at me.

I put my head in my hands. "It was so sweet."

"Oh, Brynn," she said in disappointment. "You didn't say it back, did you?"

I couldn't even look at her, so I mumbled it through my hands, "I responded with a 'that's good.'"

"Yikes."

I finally looked at her, pushing my hair back from my face. "It was so awkward this morning, I couldn't even face him."

She looked sad and disappointed, which made me cringe even more. "I just don't know what to do."

"Say it back?"

"I physically can't," I explained. "When the words try to come out, they get stuck in my throat, like my tongue stops working."

She rolled her eyes. "A little dramatic aren't we? Do you not love him?"

I thought of his sweet smile and the way he'd been fighting for me, fighting for us. How amazing he was with my family and niece and nephew. "Yes, I do."

"Then say it."

"That's the thing, I can't yet. I just…I don't know. It feels like bad luck."

"You need therapy, Brynn Clark."

That sounded like a wise idea.

Instead of facing Luke, I'd told him I didn't feel the greatest and couldn't come back over to his house. I needed a little break, a little space from everything to get my head back in order. Though that seemed like it would be a long time coming.

That therapy session was sounding pretty good right about now.

The next day, Luke called me in the morning before I got to work.

"Do you want to get lunch today? I get off early and I thought I'd swing by Feather Blue," he'd suggested.

I thought of his words, the three that were scary as shit. How could I look into his eyes again after not saying it back? I needed to say it back but I couldn't right now, which meant I couldn't see him.

"Um, I don't think I'll get lunch today, raincheck?"

"Sure," he said quietly. "Everything okay?"

"Yeah, I'm fine. Just not feeling myself," I said lamely.

"This isn't about what I said the other night, right?"

"No!" I hurriedly responded then bit my lip hard in frustration. "I…I just need a little bit of space."

He was quiet. "Space?"

"Not like…*not* like that. I just need to get my head back on straight. This isn't a breakup, I promise. I'm just…" I let out a frustrated growl. "I want to say it back to you, I do. Badly, but I can't yet."

"I get it."

I knew he didn't. If I couldn't even get it, there's no way he could. "Luke, I feel that way but I just can't get the words out." I pulled into Feather Blue and leaned my forehead on the steering wheel. "I'll come over this weekend and we can talk about it more. I think a few days to clear my head will help me be able to explain it better."

"Okay."

I hated that one word. It was an awful thing. "I'm serious Luke, this isn't a breakup or even a break, it's just Brynn working through her emotional baggage."

"I understand. I'll see you this weekend," Luke said, his voice only slightly better.

"I'll talk to you soon…bye."

I hung up and threw the phone into my purse with a swoop and sighed loudly.

Why was I so messed up? I almost ruined it between Luke and I before, I shouldn't be doing it now. But part of me couldn't get over the fact that he'd said those three scary words.

I picked up my phone and stared at it for a moment.

I could tell him, call him back and just say it. Spit it out.

I can do it this weekend when I had built my courage back up.

Yes, that's what I'll do.

The day went by in a blur at Feather Blue. We were so busy I didn't have time to check my phone or even talk to Emma much until we were closing for the night. She frowned as she looked at a text she received.

"That's weird," Emma said softly, grabbing her lunch bag from the small frig. I took mine, full of my uneaten lunch.

See, it wasn't a lie to Luke.

"What's weird?"

Emma looked puzzled and finally glanced up at me. "Sam just got called into work. He doesn't normally work nights."

I checked my phone but saw nothing from Luke. He was probably in bed or maybe just not wanting to talk to me.

Space. I'd said a bad word for any couple in a relationship.

"That is odd. Someone called off maybe?"

Emma put the phone into her pocket as we left the store. "Probably."

"At least he'll get overtime," I suggested.

She scoffed. "I'd rather have him, but it is good money."

When we got to our cars, I stopped Emma. "How…how long was it until you told him you loved him?"

She threw her stuff into the car then faced me looking sheepish. "Three weeks."

My mouth dropped. "Seriously? That soon? Is there like a timeframe I'm missing?"

"No," she said with a laugh. "Everyone is different, Brynn. Sam and I just knew, and it was the right timing."

I rubbed my temple in distress.

"Still overthinking this stuff with Luke?"

"Yes. I also screwed up but what haven't I though?'"

Emma put a hand on my arm and squeezed gently. "Luke understands or at least is trying to."

"But for how long?"

She shrugged, looking just as concerned as I felt.

I slept restlessly that night and woke up several times throughout to stare at my ceiling or check my phone. It was dumb, he wasn't going to be texting me. He was giving me the 'space' I'd wanted.

By six in the morning, I'd had enough. I was going to go see him before work. I needed to air things out between us and tell him I didn't want space. Saying the word 'space' had been a stupid idea.

I got changed and was headed out the door when I heard a car pulling into my driveway. I glanced out the window and saw the Cold Spring Police car spraying stones as they quickly pulled in.

Luke. He'd learned to not listen to me!

I opened the door with a smile on my lips, ready to leap across my porch and into his arms, but when the door of the squad car opened, it wasn't Luke.

Sam jumped out and looked at me. His crumpled shirt had specks of blood on it. His black hair was messy and his eyes...his eyes were what really worried me. They were fearful and sad.

"What's wrong?" I demanded. I couldn't move as my heart rate pummeled through my ears, making it hard to breathe or hear.

"It's Luke. He's been shot."

Chapter Four

The Risk of Loving Someone

"What?" I asked dumbly. "Sh-shot? How? Where is he?"

"We were called to Trinket's Motor to investigate a possible theft in progress. When we got there, the thieves had guns." Sam's voice broke and I saw his hands tremble. "We didn't see it coming. Luke took several shots to his vest and one caught his leg."

I felt my knees buckle, my heart sinking. "Is he okay?"

Sam's face was pale. "I don't know, he was conscious when I took him to the hospital, but the bleeding was bad."

I didn't tell him I love you. I didn't tell him that he meant everything to me. Why had I not? Would I lose my chance?

My ears still ringing, I asked, "He's at Cold Spring Hospital?"

"Yes."

Sam didn't say anything else as I ran back into the house and grabbed my keys and purse. I bolted to my car and Sam pulled out behind me as I stepped on the gas to get to the hospital.

My throat felt tight as I ran to the front doors. The receptionist looked at me as I raced up to the desk, adrenaline running through my body.

"Luke Price," were the only words that could come out. My hands shook and I felt like I was going to burst into tears.

"He's still in ICU. You can wait in there." She pointed to a small waiting area and then I felt Sam run in behind me.

The young girl looked alarmed upon seeing him. "Officer Locklear."

"How's he doing? Any word?" he asked.

She shook her head. "I just told her he's in ICU. We won't know until the doctor finishes examining him."

He nodded, looking frazzled.

"Has his father been called?" I croaked out.

The receptionist looked down at his chart. "Is that Bill Price?"

"Yes."

"No, he hasn't been called yet."

A sudden sense of fear came over me and the room began to spin at the thought of losing Luke. I couldn't lose him.

Seeing me sway, Sam guided me over to a chair and I sat down heavily in it.

"He's a tough one, Brynn. He'll be okay," Sam reassured but his voice wasn't convincing.

I stared at my shaking hands, my eyes filling with tears. "I haven't gotten to tell him I love him."

Tears broke from my eyes and Sam put a comforting arm around me. "Shit, where's Emma," he mumbled as I sobbed. A nurse came out and saw the situation and handed him a box of tissues. I grabbed the tissues and dabbed at my eyes.

"I have to call Bill," I told him, trying to compose myself.

Sam looked relieved that I wasn't crying as hard. "Maybe we should wait until the doctor comes out."

"Will they even tell us anything if we aren't one of his family members?"

Sam gave a sad smile. "Luke added me about a year ago. He didn't have anyone else and asked if I'd be willing."

Oh, thank God.

"I'll wait."

Waiting was the worst part and I belatedly realized I hadn't called Emma to tell her I wouldn't be in to work. Sam reassured me that she already knew and was coming to be with us as soon as the part time employee got there. I thanked him repeatedly.

My chest hurt from sobbing and my head pounded with a headache. My phone started going off and I quickly turned it on silent only to see the text messages start rolling in.

Kate: *We heard there was a shooting, and a few police officers were caught in it. Everyone alright?*

Dylan: *Heard about that too. I texted Luke to make sure he was okay but he hasn't texted back.*

Mark: *Let us know. Dad and Mom are worried too.*

Lauren: *Nothing like this happens in Cold Spring! Like what the heck!*

My stomach tightened as I responded.

Me: *It was Luke. He's in ICU. I'm at the hospital now waiting to hear. Don't call me though because I don't know if I can talk without crying.*

Instead of waiting for responses, I turned my phone off.

A few seconds later, a doctor came out and called Sam's name. We both stood up and I felt my heart pounding hard in my chest.

"Is he okay?" Sam asked before the doctor could say anything more.

"He's stable. The bullet went into his calf but luckily didn't sever his artery. He should be fine in a few days but he will need to rest and go through some physical therapy. We're going to get him settled into a room and after that, you'll be able to visit."

I let out a relieved sob and Sam put a hand on my shoulder to steady me.

"Thank you," Sam said, relief filling him too.

The doctor looked serious for a moment. "If you hadn't gotten him here as quickly as you did, this might have ended worse. Your quick action saved him."

Sam didn't say anything, just nodded.

The doctor left us, and Sam and I sat down again.

I should have told him how much I loved him. I almost lost my chance to tell him that, but I was done keeping my feelings back. I was going to show Luke Price just how much he meant to me because I could lose him in a moment.

"Did you arrest the people who did this?" I asked Sam whose fingers were flying over his phone.

"Yes. Two men came from New York City trying to steal catalytic converters. This isn't their first offense. They were both taken to jail."

I turned my phone back on feeling only slightly better. "I'm going to call Bill."

Sam nodded and I walked outside of the hospital to get some air and to calm my beating heart.

Bill answered after a few rings.

"Brynn, how are you?" Bill said, sounding surprised.

"Hey Bill, I..." I trailed off, not sure what exactly to say.

"What's going on?" Bill knew by the tone of my voice that something wasn't right. I wasn't any good at this! How was I supposed to tell him what happened?

"Bill, Luke was shot but he's okay. He was shot in the leg. The doctor just came out to tell us that he's recovering and will be okay."

"Oh," Bill said, his voice hoarse. "The boy can't keep out of trouble."

I could tell he was trying not to sound upset but I read right through it. "We're at the Cold Spring Hospital. I can meet you outside when you get here."

After calling and talking to my mom about Luke, I asked her to tell everyone else so I didn't have to. She and Dad both sounded upset and worried.

By the time I got back into the hospital, the nurses were ready to take us to Luke's room. I started to walk with them and noticed Sam didn't follow.

"You aren't coming?"

Sam held his hat in his hands. "No, I'll wait for Emma. Go on ahead."

I did without thinking about it. I needed to see him. I had to touch him and make sure he was okay.

The nurse guided me into a room. The first bed was empty but in the one beside the windows lay a sleeping man.

My heart plummeted as I saw that the sleeping man was Luke. His hair was pushed back and there was an IV line attached to his hand. He was wearing a hospital gown and his left leg was propped up on pillows and covered.

I slowly walked toward him as the nurse shut the door behind me. I wiped my sweaty hands on my pants as I quietly moved closer so I could fully look him over. He seemed fine, his face wasn't pinched in pain and his heart monitor had a steady beat.

Black eyelashes framed his closed eyes, and I watched them slowly flutter open. Brown eyes took a moment until they focused on me and when he saw me, his lip tweaked into a half smile.

"Want to buy me a beer?" he croaked.

I half laughed, half sobbed as I ran to his side and hugged him tightly. He smelled of antiseptic and blood.

"I'm so glad you're okay!"

I put my head over his chest and squeezed, thanking God Luke was still here with me.

"I'm fine," he tried to reassure but when I lifted my head to look at him, I glared.

"Did you really have to go get shot to hear me say I love you?"

His eyes lit up with joy. "Are you saying what I think you're saying?"

I took his open palm and put it against my cheek. "Yes, Luke, I love you."

It didn't freak me out and it didn't make me worry like it had the day before. I felt nothing but true love for him.

His expression grew serious. "This is the risk of being with me, Brynn. This could happen again. It doesn't worry you?"

I let his hand go from my cheek but kept it pressed tightly with mine. "No, Luke. It makes me want to love you harder."

He liked that answer, and he pulled me gently down until we kissed lightly on the lips. I leaned back to touch his cheek, his long nose, his rumpled hair until I finally put my head back on his chest and breathed in deeply.

I almost lost him today. I'd almost lost the chance to tell him how much he meant to me and that I did really love him. I would risk whatever I had to just to be with Luke.

"I called your dad. He's coming soon," I whispered against his chest.

He sighed. "Great."

"I'd smack you, but I think you've been through enough for today."

"He's going to lecture me about being safe."

Bill came a little bit later and I walked him back to Luke's room. When he saw Luke, he just stopped, and I could feel emotions hitting him.

"Hey Dad," Luke said softly. "I don't know what she told you but I'm fine."

I rolled my eyes at being thrown under the bus. Bill walked forward and I stood waiting at the door, unsure what to do.

"You need to be more careful, son. This job is no joke," Bill's voice choked but Luke still glared at me over his shoulder.

"It's just a bullet to the leg. I'm okay."

"Oh yeah? Who's to say next time it won't be worse?"

Luke sighed and scratched his forehead, the IV line bobbing with the movement.

"Dad."

"You've got Brynn now, Luke. You can't be taking risks."

Luke's annoyance had died off as I stood there awkwardly behind them.

Bill thought of me? He was thinking about us? How much did Luke talk about me?

"Dad, I wasn't. It was two thieves stealing catalytic converters. We weren't prepared."

His dad's demeanor changed. "Well son, I'd say you're getting rusty then."

Luke chuckled and I even cracked a smile. I walked over to the two and I saw Bill had his hand on Luke's forearm.

"Bill, are you planning to stay? I can get the spare room ready in Luke's house for you."

He smiled kindly at me. "I'll stay a few days. I have Barney in the car with me."

"No, you know how I feel about dogs in my house," Luke cut in, but Bill just waved a hand at him.

"Barney is a good dog. He won't hurt nothing."

Luke rolled his eyes skyward and the muscles in his neck bulged.

"I'll take Barney back and get the house ready. You can stay here with Luke," I suggested.

Bill looked happy with that but Luke didn't. I didn't want to leave him either but I knew I wanted to make sure Bill was comfortable and Luke didn't want to worry about anything.

"I'll come back," I promised Luke as I leaned down to kiss his lips. We lingered for just a moment and as I pulled back I whispered. "I love you."

"I love you too," he responded. His hand stayed on my leg for as long as it could until I left the room.

Emma and Sam were in the waiting room, and they stood when they saw me. "He's doing fine. Bill is with him," I announced.

"Good," Sam said as Emma reached to pull me into a hug.

"I'm sorry I didn't get here earlier. I had to wait until Sophie got in. She had to get a babysitter."

"It's alright, Em. I'm going back to Luke's to take care of some stuff. I'll be back here in a little while."

She kissed my cheek and I left.

Chapter Five

Barney the Bastard

When I got out to my car, I unlocked it and saw Barney sitting in Bill's red Chevy with his head out the window and his tail wagging.

"Hi buddy," I called. He gave a happy bark as I walked over and glanced in the window. I saw his leash was attached. "Wanna come with me?"

He looked so thrilled, he gave another bark and his tail hit a plastic cup in Bill's cup holder. I opened the door and grabbed the leash as he jumped out of the truck. He then leaped into the back seat of my car. Barney was way too trusting.

When we got to Luke's, I found the spare key and opened the door with Barney in tow. I let go of the leash to fill up a bowl of water for him as I hurried to change the sheets on the guest bed and even plugged in the alarm clock for Bill. It was something I'd seen Luke do for him when he visited.

When I finished with the guest room, I went into the bathroom to put my hair up and groaned. I should've kept my hair stuff here! Why was I such an idiot?

Ignoring my self-pity, I listened and realized I didn't hear anything.

"Barney?" I called out. I heard the thunderous paws as he hit the stairs two at a time to come to my voice. When I met him in the hall, I saw he was licking his chops.

Oh no.

I ran down the stairs and there on the floor of the kitchen was a loaf of half eaten bread.

"You brat! No wonder Luke doesn't want you here!"

Barney's tail wagged as if he had no idea what I was talking about and his golden eyes shined with love. "Good thing you're cute."

I decided to run to the grocery store and get Luke a new loaf of bread along with some food for Bill. I didn't want him to have to search for things to eat. I wasn't sure how long he was planning to stay. I ended up locking Barney in the bathroom to ensure he didn't get into anything else knowing Luke would be pissed.

At the store, I was stopped several times by people who heard what happened to Luke and were concerned. I let them know he was recovering and thanked them for asking. I grabbed a chew toy for Barney, a rotisserie chicken for Bill, and several other things to help him during his stay.

Before I went in the house, I called Bill to see how Luke was.

"He's fine," he reassured me. "Not listening very well so you'll need to come back and whip him into shape."

"Not sure if that's possible, Bill," I said with a laugh.

"Nurse says visiting hours are until eight and not open again until nine tomorrow."

"I'm just going to drop this stuff off at the house and I'll be over."

"Sounds good, dear."

I carried the bags of groceries into the house and put all the cold stuff away. I took out the toy and headed upstairs to get Barney. When I came around the corner, I saw the light had somehow turned off in the bathroom. I opened the door, flipped on the light, and found a disaster. The curtain rod from the shower was bent laying of the floor and the curtain itself was ripped in several pieces. A half-eaten bar of soap was in pieces on the rug. And the rug? On the rug was a large pile of dog barf. How did I know it was dog barf? Kibble and bits of soap in a foaming mess.

Barney sat there, staring at me with wide innocent eyes as his tail beat on the floor.

My shoulders slumped in defeat. "Barney! Luke is going to kill me!"

I cleaned up the mess Barney made, throwing out the white rug and the shower curtain. I quickly called the local vet to make sure Barney was okay after eating soap, though he was more likely to be strangled by me than killed by the soap.

The vet, Dr. Skyler McCauslin, who grew up in town, told me Barney should be fine as long as he had thrown up most of it and was acting normal. I even read her off the ingredients from the soap package just to make sure. She assured me he would be fine. When I thanked her repeatedly and hung up, the little shit was sitting there staring at me with his lips pulled up as if he was smiling. He was fine.

Thank God.

The last thing I wanted to do was kill my boyfriend’s dad's dog. That would surely get me kicked out of the Price family for good.

I went to close the door after having put up anything that he could steal off the counters or try to eat, put some water and food down and glared at him.

“If you mess up anything more, I’m never going to get you a toy ever again.”

He dropped the plastic duck from his mouth where it squealed on the floor.

I shut the door and headed back to the hospital.

Bill was lounging in the recliner, across from Luke who was now sitting up, reading over a newspaper.

“Ah, there she is. How’s my buddy doing?” Bill asked.

I thought perhaps it was a joke considering the hell I'd just gone through and even Luke looked at me expectantly.

Through my teeth, I answered, "He's fine."

I was going to have to subtly get a new rug and shower curtain for the bathroom though. *Thank you, Bill.*

I went to the edge of the bed and looked over a pale Luke. He seemed to be in a little more pain than he had been, and I put my hand on his forehead. He felt slightly warm, and he smiled at my care.

"How are you feeling, baby?"

His eyes twinkled at that even though pain laced them.

"Do you want some pain medicine?"

"You know when I almost lost this finger," Bill said, waving his right index finger in the air. "I didn't need any painkillers."

"I know, Dad," Luke said with a grimace. I saw the plea in his eyes, and I went over to Bill.

"I got some food for you at the house. If you want to head back, go ahead. I'll stay here until visiting hours are over."

And go get your shithead of a dog too. That part I kept quiet.

"I think that sounds like a good idea," Bill said, sitting up, He stared out the door but paused to look back at me. "Thanks dear, for taking care of our boy."

That may have possibly made up for his dog puking soap all over Luke's floor and me having to clean it. Almost.

"You're welcome, Bill."

He shut the door quietly behind him and I went over to sit on the edge of the bed so I could touch Luke's hand.

His forehead was creased in pain. "I'm sorry for throwing all of this on—"

"Don't. It's okay. I would do anything you ask."

He grimaced as a wave of pain washed through him. His leg shifted and he paled.

"We can call the nurse in—"

"No. I'm fine."

I rolled my eyes. "You just got shot, Luke, now isn't the time to be macho."

"I'm not," he countered through clenched teeth. "I can deal with it. My dad did, I should be able to."

I raised a brow but didn't fuss. "Tell me what happened," I whispered.

He sighed and leaned his head back on the pillow. The tendons in his neck pulsed from the pain but then he breathed in a deep breath and exhaled.

"Sam and I picked up the night shift since a few of the guys were out because of a stomach bug. Sam thought the overtime would help with the wedding, so I volunteered with him." I held his hand tighter, and he held mine back. "Martha Trinket called us because she saw flashlights in the back by the garage. When we got there, we didn't see their car, but we found the guys under one of the trucks, taking off a converter. We spooked them and next thing you know they started shooting at us. We hid behind one of the other cars, but we didn't get to cover quick enough." He rubbed his chest subconsciously until I saw him wince.

"You wore your vest?"

He nodded and pulled up his gown and I saw several bruises. I gasped and touched one with my fingertips. "Luke," I whispered.

"The vest stops the bullet from penetrating, but it still does some damage. I took more hits in the drug raid."

There were two; one beside his heart, the other right above his belly button. "That would have killed you if you didn't have your vest on," I whispered as tears filled my eyes.

"They were sporadic shots. Luckily, we caught the two men as soon as backup came, and they were arrested." He sighed and then flinched. He was too hard-headed to ask for medicine.

"I have to run out to my car, I'll be right back," I said.

"What?" he demanded, seeming upset.

"I have gummy worms."

He perked up at that. He was a grown man, but his favorite candy was gummy worms. I learned

“We’re so glad he’s okay. Bill just updated us.” She pulled back to dab at her eyes.

Mark was next to pull me in for a fatherly hug.

“Bill,” I said unsteadily. “This is my brother Mark and sister, Kate.”

He waved a hand with a smile. “Don’t worry dear, they introduced themselves. They were actually here looking for you. Brought us some food,” he said with a shake of the container. It took me a moment to remember I hadn’t eaten anything today. My stomach had been in knots so badly I couldn’t keep anything down.

“That’s so nice of you guys, here come inside.”

Bill cleared his throat, getting my attention, and leaned down to me. “Um, Barney might have ripped apart a pillow. I was in the midst of cleaning it up when they arrived.”

I sighed. “It’s fine. They have two kids and they destroy more than pillows.”

“It’s true,” Mark announced.

We all went in together and I took the container Kate brought to the kitchen. It was her famous macaroni salad that I loved.

Barney came skirting into the house and ran and jumped right onto the couch.

I stared in horror at the sight. Oh my God.

Bill rushed him off the couch. Kate and Mark stood around the kitchen with me.

"Bill was just saying he was awake and talking just fine," Kate said as Mark put a hand on her shoulder.

"Yes, he's awake and in pain but okay. There were several shots fired," I paused to steady my voice. "He was shot multiple times and all but one were in his vest. The one hit his leg. It missed an artery, thank God."

"What the hell happened over there?" Mark asked quietly.

Bill was seated in the living room watching the news with Barney panting happily at his side. He had a cup of coffee in his hands.

"Luke said it was two guys who were stealing catalytic converters. It wasn't anyone local," I answered, biting my nail.

"No one else was hurt?" Kate asked.

"Only Luke. They arrested the two and they will be prosecuted."

Mark blew out his breath and ran a hand through his hair. "Cold Spring doesn't see stuff like this."

"I know," I said quietly.

Kate saw my exhausted expression and rubbed my arm. "We just wanted to see how you were doing. We were hoping to maybe stop into the hospital with the kiddos once Luke is feeling up to it."

"I'll let you know. Where are the kids?"

"At Mom and Dad's. They were there after school today and we asked them to keep them until we got done here," Mark said.

"Thank you," I breathed.

Kate hugged me tightly and Mark was next. "Call us if you need something, Sis," Mark said as they were leaving. I waved from the porch and luckily blocked Barney from escaping with my leg.

I shut the door, and he trotted over to Bill who sat chuckling at a late night TV show.

He seemed unfazed by everything going on and I still felt like a spigot about to burst. I sat down on the sofa and Barney came over to set his head on my lap. I still petted him, even if I was pissed at what he'd ruined.

"Barney destroyed the shower curtain and the rug in the bathroom. I bought the new ones to replace them," I announced over the TV.

Bill winced and looked over. "Should've warned you about that one. Did he try to eat the hand towels?"

I wish I had a beer.

"No, the soap."

Make it a vodka.

He flinched. "I'll tell Luke—"

"I think it would be best if we didn't. The last thing I want is for him to have a heart attack." I sighed and closed my eyes, leaning back on the couch. I heard him munching on something and peeked open an eye to see he'd collected the mixed nuts I'd bought and was snacking on them. He threw one to Barney who snatched it out of the air.

"You don't seem worried about Luke," I mentioned.

He didn't even look my way as he popped another handful of nuts into his mouth and munched as he talked. "That's because my son is a police officer. This isn't the first time he's been shot at and if he stays in this profession, it won't be the last." He finally looked over and for a moment I saw fear in his gaze. "His mother worried herself sick about him and prayed every day that God would protect him. It comes with loving someone whose life could be over during their nine-to-five job. I'm afraid you'll have to get used to it, Dear." He turned back towards the TV and laughed at something, rubbing his salty hands onto the couch arm.

Luke was going to kill me.

I woke with a start and looked around the dark living room. The lights had been shut off and there was a blanket draped over me. Barney was gone too, and I assumed he was up in bed with Bill.

I glanced around the dark room and realized how empty it was without Luke. It felt weird to be here without him coming around the corner with a smile. It was too late to drive home, and I honestly wanted to be here.

I trudged up the stairs and into Luke's bedroom. I slipped on his signature sweats and white t-shirt and crawled right into bed. I even scooted over onto his side so I could still feel like he was right beside me.

Chapter Six

I Smell Chanel #5

Luke was in the hospital for a week. Many people from Cold Spring visited to wish him well and say thank you. My family also visited. Mark and Kate brought the kids and Bailey had drawn him a picture and brought dandelions. Luke had especially liked that. My parents dropped off food at Luke's house to feed Bill, me, and unfortunately Barney, who somehow got cookies off the counter and thoroughly enjoyed them.

Asshole dog.

When Luke was finally released, I drove him home in my car. He seemed in good spirits and not in as much pain.

"Is my dad staying tonight?"

I really wanted to say "I hope not," but decided that would be rude. I liked Bill a lot, but Barney was the spawn of the devil and the last thing I wanted was for Luke to see the chaos he brought. "I'm not sure. I'll ask when we get back."

"He said you cooked for him this week," Luke said, putting a hand on my leg. His hair had grown longer and his beard was almost full. He hadn't been able to shave and I honestly wanted him to keep it. It was fitting on him, like a lumberjack or a rogue FBI agent.

"I made a few meals, but it my family brought over most of them."

"I appreciate it, Brynn."

I smiled over at him and couldn't help but feel relieved he was coming home.

"Have they told you when you can go back to work?"

He hated that question because his boss had put him on paid leave for six weeks and told him not to come back unless he felt good enough. Well, he felt good enough now, but everyone told him no. He was not one to care about wounds and how he felt, his job was his life.

"As of now, no."

Luke leaned some of his weight on me as I helped him out of the car. He paused to take a breath and regain his footing and stared at the front door.

I bit my lip as I quietly said to him, "Emma put her house up on the market yesterday. Apparently, there's already a few offers."

He went still but didn't glance over at me. "Oh yeah?"

"It's a nice place, but I just don't think it's me. I told her I wasn't going to make an offer."

He finally looked at me and I saw hopefulness in his gaze.

I had decided a while ago that I wouldn't buy her house. After Luke's accident, I felt myself change and that meant my commitment issues were at least hiding at the moment.

We didn't say anything more about the Emma's place as I helped him walk the rest of the way into the house. Bill opened the front door with a happy smile on his face. He held Barney back so he didn't come running and knock us over.

"Hey, son! You look better."

Luke just grunted in response. When we made it into the house, he paused to take a breath and I gasped. The kitchen was filled with different trays, bowls, and bags filled with food. Sitting next to them were several bouquets of flowers.

"Bill! Where did all this come from?"

Luke stared in awe just like me.

"The towns folk. Really nice people, Luke you've made quite an impression on them," Bill added.

Maybe they weren't all gossiping mongrels. They cared.

Still holding onto Luke, I looked at him. "Upstairs?"

He nodded, already seeming exhausted. Side by side, we went up the stairs one step at a time. "Should we add a wheelchair ramp?" I joked.

He grunted a curse word at me which made me chuckle. Once we got to the hallway, he put a hand on the wall and took a moment to catch his breath. Sweat beaded on his head. I felt awful and wished I could've done something.

"I need a beer," he muttered slightly out of breath.

"You can't mix that with painkillers," I scolded.

He looked into the bathroom, and I saw his features change.

Oh shit.... did he see that Barney had literally destroyed the bathroom?

"You changed the rug and shower curtain," he said, with a hopefulness in his voice. He looked back at met and he was smiling.

Oh. "Yeah, I thought it needed updating."

"I like it." He leaned forward and kissed me. "Brynn, I want you to make this place how you want it. You're welcome to keep doing that."

Well, buddy, I may have to redo the entire house unless your father takes the devil dog away.

I already was going to have to replace the pillows in the living room since Barney had used them as chew toys. The duck toy I'd purchased was barely touched.

"Thanks, I will."

I didn't care that he didn't know it wasn't me that caused the curtain and rug change. It meant something to him and honestly, it didn't bother me one bit about anything he'd said. It didn't give me a pang of fear or a worry about commitment.

Well, this was a step in the right direction. Maybe

Luke just had to get shot for me to start feeling this way.

I got him settled into bed and as I went back downstairs, Bill had his bag and Barney at the front door.

"You're leaving?" I asked.

"Yep, I think I'll let you tend to him until he's better," Bill said. He stepped closer to me and put a hand on my shoulder, growing serious. "Thank you for what you've given him. He's got hope because of you."

I felt tears fill my eyes at his words. "He's given me hope too."

He liked that answer and nodded his head. "Take care of our boy, I'll be calling to check in soon."

I waved to him and Barney from the porch and went back inside. I filled a plate for Luke with food from all the containers in the kitchen. There were so many different kinds of meat, sides dishes, desserts…the town had really stepped up and I was thankful for them.

I took the plate of food upstairs to him. The TV was already on, and he was watching the news. He smiled softly as I put the plate onto his lap and sat his water on the tableside stand.

"I got you a little of everything."

He took a bite of some coleslaw and focused on the TV.

I went to my bag sitting by his dresser and rifled through it trying to locate some clothes. I should just leave stuff here.

"Do you have a drawer I could use?"

He looked over, spoon midway to his mouth, and looked surprised. "Bottom one is empty."

I opened the bottom drawer of his dresser and put my things in it. I knew right then that it had been cleaned out a while ago…waiting for me to fill it.

Sneaky, lying man.

I finished and changed into comfortable clothes, but I felt him staring at my back. I peeked over my shoulder to see him watching me very intently.

"Can I help you?" I asked slyly.

"Turn around."

I did, slowly, and let him get his fill before I finished throwing my shirt on and pants.

He sighed in disappointment as I came to sit beside him.

"You know—" he started.

"You are not healed enough for that yet," I cut him off with a *tisk*.

"I can be on bottom," he argued.

I laughed and ate a brownie from his plate then curled up next to him.

"Not until you're healed more."

He did a very dramatic head roll into the pillow with a groan, and I couldn't help but chuckle.

Emma let me off work for several days to take care of Luke. She'd told me to take as much time as I needed.

Sam stopped by every other day to check on him and I tried to give them privacy to chat knowing they were talking about work. Sam seemed upset every time he left and not his happy self. So finally, I asked Luke. "What's wrong with him? Are he and Emma okay?"

Luke had ventured downstairs on his own and limped into the kitchen.

"Yeah, he's fine. Just dealing with work stuff," Luke reassured me not making eye contact.

I walked over to him as he popped a handful of mixed nuts into his mouth reminding me a lot of his dad.

"What aren't you telling me?" I narrowed my eyes.

He hated the look I was giving him. It was motherly and probably condescending.

"He feels it's his fault I got shot."

"Why?"

Luke looked away and took a drink of water. "Because I pushed him out of the way when I heard the first shot."

My jaw dropped and I felt my heart constrict at his words. "You pushed Sam out of the way to take the hit?"

He finally looked at me and I saw resolve in his gaze. "It was automatic and the last thing I wanted was for Emma to not have a groom on her wedding day."

He'd been upset at me that day too. Had I pushed him to do that? Pushed him to risk his life because Sam had more to live for? Or had the ex-NYPO just done what he would have done any day for one of his partners?

Luke went on, not realizing I was deep in thought. "He wants to tell the station about it and make me his best man," he gave an annoyed wave. "I don't want to deal with all that shit. He saved my life by getting me to the hospital quickly, but he doesn't see that."

I was still trying to comprehend everything he'd said and was still very much focused on the fact that he'd saved Sam.

He saved Sam. He pushed him out of the way and risked his own life to save Sam's. Luke was an amazing man. I was at a loss for words.

I walked up to him and he sighed, seeing something in my eyes and preparing for it. Instead of scolding, I kissed him.

It was the first deep—gave you all the feels—kiss we'd had since the shooting. He wrapped his arms tightly around me and pressed our bodies together. I pulled him to the couch and made him sit as I started taking off his shirt. He didn't question where this came from or why I was doing it and since it'd been over two weeks since we'd had sex, he probably wasn't willing to risk opening his mouth and ending it before it started.

I straddled him and leaned down to say quietly, "Let me know if your leg starts hurting,"

"No way," he said quickly and pulled my head down to kiss him fervently.

When I talked to Emma, she said Sam told her what Luke had done and that Sam was feeling guilty. Luke, of course, in Luke fashion, didn't want anything from Sam and would rather it be brushed under the rug which upset Sam. I told her I thought I could convince him to be the best man, it could be a few weeks though.

I took Luke to his physical therapy appointments each week and slowly he regained the strength in his leg as it healed. The doctor was convinced he might even get rid of his limp. I didn't leave his side except for a few days to go back and check on Felix. I felt so guilty for leaving him so I pitched the idea to Luke to allow me to bring him here so he wasn't alone. He seemed to be okay with that if it meant I was here. I'd taken up the full dresser in the room and even part of the closet but that meant my things were split half and half which was annoying.

Luke loved me being there all the time and I grew used to it as well. It was so nice to come home to him.

After working at Feather Blue for a few hours, I went back to my house to get Felix and a few things. As I collected his toys and food there was a knock at my door.

Wonder if it was Mom coming to check on Felix? I'd asked her to stop in if she could.

When I opened the door, I was stunned to find the person I never expected to see at my door.

Pam Rally, Owen's mother.

"You've got to be kidding me!" I said in exasperation. "I don't have that disgusting vase anymore. I broke it against the wall."

Pam was your pristine country club woman who wore tennis skirts and brimmed hats and Chanel #5 with Gucci shoes. Today though she was dressed in jeans and a white cashmere sweater and her blonde hair was styled perfectly. She had no gray hair and had spent thousands of dollars to keep it that way.

I hadn't seen this woman in the two years or since the divorce. It was as if when Owen decided he wanted a divorce, she wanted nothing to do with me.

Her eyes had a spike of anger in them as she heard about the vase. "I'm not here about the vase," she clipped. "Though you're lucky I never sued you for that. It was in my family for generations."

I crossed my arms and stared at her. "Then why are you here?"

"May I come in?"

"No."

She looked offended. "My blouse is going to smell of exhaust from all these cars going by. Brynn, let me in."

I didn't feel inclined to do as she asked but I was more curious as to know why she was here, so I stepped aside and let her in. She seemed to brush off something from her sleeve and looked around the house with a raised lip. "I see your tastes haven't changed."

"If you don't tell me why you're here, you're going right back out there," I snapped.

She straightened and put on a rather forced smile. "Owen wants you to come back."

"I'm sorry, I don't think I heard you right. Maybe the exhaust you were talking about filled my ears. What did you say?"

"Owen isn't good right now and needs you back. He knows he's made mistakes—"

"Several might I add, and all of them had long legs and fake boobs," I said, feeling my anger rise at this conversation.

"He regrets what he did and feels sorry about everything," she continued as if she didn't hear my last sentence.

I stared at her, realizing she was serious. She was here for her son? The son who had cheated multiple times and who I'd punched in the courthouse? Was she an idiot?

"Did you drink that Chanel #5 before bathing in it?" I demanded.

She looked appalled. "Excuse me?"

"Because you have to be drunk or on crack to think I would ever take your son back!"

She narrowed her eyes on me. "You would be wise to take him back. He brought money into your life and you didn't live in a filthy little shack like this!"

I stepped closer to her, no longer caring about what she or her idiot husband thought of me. She was my *ex-mother-in-law*. When Owen and I had dated, I had cared too much about what she'd thought of me. I cared so much that I let her rule my life and the things in it. Not anymore.

"This is my home," I said quietly. "I've built what I have after your son left me with nothing. I've met someone and he didn't come from wealthy parents who babied him his entire life. I would rather chop off my hand than ever get back together with Owen Rally."

She raised her lip. "You and I both know he deserves better than you but I'm doing this for him.

We never thought you were good enough, but we helped him buy that ring and we paid for your wedding because we thought it would work."

"So did I, Pam. But your son couldn't control where he put his dick!" It was crude and my mother would've killed me for speaking that way, but Pam was on my last nerve.

She sniffed and tried not to look offended, but I saw right through it. She knew her son was a man whore.

"I think you need to reconsider your options. You don't have money and you're almost in your thirties. Your childbearing days are limited."

I felt my ears heat with anger as I walked to my front door and opened it.

"Pam, I'm going to say this as nicely as possible," I took a deep breath, exhaled, and centered my gaze on her. "I will never, ever get back together with Owen. I have moved on and am with someone, and for once I'm happy. Now, you can leave before I even go into the whole childbearing years comment."

She pouted her red lips and slowly walked out. She paused on the step and turned to look at me with a glare.

"If you don't get back with him, we'll sue you for assault."

I laughed loudly and she looked shocked. "Oh Pam, did you forget that I'm a paralegal? I will rip you to shreds in court."

She didn't like that her plan hadn't worked. She huffed and went to her car, her heels slipping on the gravel.

"Pam!" I called with a grin. She stopped to glare. "Thanks for the engagement ring. I pawned it to get a haircut and some drinks!"

I called my mom right away and told her what had happened. She was just as livid and we vented for hours.

I had decided I wasn't going to tell Luke about it because it was just an annoying ex-mother-in-law, or monster-in-law. Even Mom agreed that in Luke's condition, it wasn't a good idea.

“This is going to make me sound like a horrible person, but I don’t care. I'm relieved that if Luke and I ever progress into marriage, I won’t have a mother-in-law. Does that make me sound like a bad person?”

Mom laughed. “No, honey. It makes Luke even more attractive!”

Chapter Seven

One Ring to Rule My Thoughts

A few months passed and Felix and I stayed at Luke's regularly. Felix had taken to the house easily, just like I thought he would.

Luke had started back to work on light duty, six weeks on the dot. He was getting used to working behind the desk but was annoyed with paperwork already.

Pam Rally was out of my mind and thoughts completely after her unexpected visit. It made me grateful to have only Bill to deal with. And unfortunately, Barney.

I finished folding our clothes and started putting them away. I thought it would be nice if I did it for Luke. I opened a few of his drawers and put the jeans and T-shirts away and then I paused. In his top drawer, I stared at a small navy-colored box. Not just any box...a *ring* box.

My heart wanted to leap out of my chest as I stared at it. I felt my adrenaline spike as I reached for it and opened the small box. When the lid popped, I jumped.

It was a beautiful ring...not just a one-diamond ring but three little diamonds on a silver band. It was stunning. A little flashy but still delicate.

Luke was planning to propose? When did he buy it? We never really talked about getting married.

Oh God...what if I didn't want to get remarried?

After all my past problems, I wasn't sure if I wanted to. I definitely wasn't ready! *Not now.*

I snapped the lid shut and put it back in the drawer as my ears rang.

I grabbed the clothes basket and ran downstairs to throw it in the laundry room and collect my keys. My thoughts were solely on the ring as I got in the car and drove to Feather Blue. When I walked in the front door, Emma just rolled her eyes.

"Brynn, you're supposed to be off today," she complained.

I went behind the counter, grabbed her arm, and hauled her to the back room.

"What is going on?" she demanded as I shut the office door.

"I found a ring," I stated, my voice shaking.

Emma crossed her arms looking confused. "What do you mean?"

I started pacing, walking back and forth in the tight office space. "I was putting Luke's clothes away and when I opened a drawer there was a ring box…Emma, *a ring box*!"

Her eyes grew wide as she finally understood what I was saying. "Oh!"

"Yes! It's silver with three diamonds on it and very flashy but simple." I continued pacing, my hand going to my head which felt hot.

Was I having a panic attack?

"Ooh! When Sam and I were at Swan's Jewelry the other day looking for wedding bands, I saw one like that!" When I just stared at her in horror, she added, "Brynn, Luke is going to propose!"

Hearing that made my stomach roll with anxiety and excitement. I wasn't sure which one I preferred. "I don't know what to do, Em! I don't know if I even want to get remarried!"

Her expression changed, realizing my dilemma. "Have you guys talked about it?"

"No! Absolutely not. We've only been together six months. I didn't think it would happen this soon."

"Do you think him getting shot made him want to make your relationship more concrete?"

I finally threw myself down into one of the chairs, sighed loudly, and put my head into my hands. "No, he's been shot several times before this," I mumbled. "I mean I love him a lot. I'd marry him…eventually, but I don't know if that eventually is *now*."

Emma nodded, understanding me as no one else did.

I'd just gotten the nerve to leave a freaking toothbrush at my boyfriend's house a few months ago and it took me three months and a bullet to his leg to say *I love you* to him. I remembered him telling me that his first girlfriend said no when he'd proposed to her. Would he chance that again with me?

"If I said not now, would he stay with me?" I asked quietly, looking up at Emma.

Her expression said it all. *No, he wouldn't.* I needed to say yes or lose Luke forever.

A few weeks passed and I still hadn't convinced myself that I would say yes. I practiced stupidly in front of the mirror, but I couldn't cover up my look of horror and fear.

One evening I got back from work late, Luke had made dinner and set the table, and even poured wine. I stood there dumbly, my lunch box still in hand as he flipped two large steaks in a skillet.

He grinned at me. "Hi, sweetie."

"Hi."

I looked around suspiciously, thinking maybe I'd see the ring box just sitting somewhere but no.

Was this the night?

I slowly walked into the kitchen and Luke met me halfway to kiss me deeply, his hand ghosting around my back to draw me in.

When he let go, he smiled down with those twinkling brown eyes.

"You're happy."

"I had a good day at work," he shrugged and went back to the steaks. "Go get changed into something comfortable and hurry back. These are almost done."

I did as he asked, my hands starting to shake.

Would my family be here? Shit, that's what Owen had done when he proposed. He'd done this grand gesture with our families' present, and I had hated it.

I glanced out the bathroom window to check the side yard to make sure no cars sat there, and it was empty.

I changed into sweats and pulled off my jewelry. I kept staring at the drawer in the bedroom, wondering if he had it in his pocket but I didn't have the nerve to go look.

When I got back downstairs, he'd filled our plates and gestured to my chair to sit.

"How's your leg feeling?" I asked, taking a bite of my steak.

"Better. Doesn't even feel like I got shot," he said.

My hands slightly shook, and I gave up trying to eat and downed the majority of my wine. I couldn't deal with this anymore.

"So, what's this about?"

A bite of steak was midway to his mouth when he paused. "What's *what* about?"

I gestured to the table and wine, even him who looked delicious wearing jeans and a plain tee.

"Dinner, wine…all of it?"

He put down his knife and fork and his brows furrowed. "Can't I make dinner for my girlfriend?"

I swallowed at his expression.

Maybe he wasn't going to? Maybe I'd read this wrong.

"Yes."

"Maybe I wanted to thank you for being there by my side through my recovery. I couldn't have done it without you." His sincere words made my heart leap and I reached across the table to take his solid, warm hand.

"I'm sorry, I'm just not myself today," I mumbled.

He smiled and I watched his hand reach for his right pocket and I jumped up from the table, knocking over my wine. "Shit! Shit!" It dribbled down onto the floor and Luke and I grabbed a towel to clean it before it stained. As we sat on the floor, cleaning up the wine, Luke laughed.

"It's fine, Brynn. I have a stain remover."

I glanced at his pocket and saw there wasn't anything in it.

Had I freaked out for nothing?

He pulled me to my feet and sat back down at the table. "Just eat, we'll worry about it later."

I felt stupid, so ridiculously stupid, but then again how was that different from any other day?

"Brynn, I did want to talk to you about something," Luke said, taking a swig of his wine.

I looked up in panic, my eyes wide and my heart rate increasing. "Wh-what?"

His smile was soft and a little nervous.

Here it was. *Would I be able to keep the horror off my face? Would it show*? If it did, I would lose him.

"I wanted to see how you felt about moving in with me?"

It took me at least thirty seconds to actually register what he said. "What?"

"I'd like you to move in with me. Felix, too, of course. Over the last few months, you've practically lived here anyhow. I know your lease is up soon."

At that point, moving in sounded way less scary than getting married.

"Oh." I was shocked to feel a pang of disappointment.

Disappointment? Brynn! He isn't proposing! Well…yet. There was still a hidden ring.

"Just oh?" Luke asked, prodding.

I cleared my thoughts and smiled at him. "I think I would like to do that."

He grinned then and it was just a beautiful, breath-taking smile that made my stomach warm.

"Great!" He leaned across the table and kissed me.

An hour later I hunkered down beside the shower and called Emma.

"Did he do it?" she answered without saying the 'hello.'

"No! He asked me to move in with him."

"Oh, well, that's not what we were expecting, but what are you thinking?"

"Well, yes. I'm going to move in with him. Honestly, that seems less scary than getting remarried."

She chuckled. "Oh, Brynn."

There was a knock at the door.

"Sweetheart, are you okay?" Luke asked, sounding concerned.

"Yes, just taking off my makeup!" I called back. I heard him walk away and let out a breath of relief. "I just don't understand why he bought the ring then. What is he waiting on?"

"For you to finally want to get married?" she suggested with a hint of sarcasm.

I rolled my eyes and realized she couldn't see me. "I don't know when that will be! All those divorce books didn't warn me about getting remarried. They never said I would have this many commitment issues!"

"Did you ever actually read them?"

I pressed my lips together and murmured, "No, not really, but I got the gist of them."

She laughed. "Brynn, stop thinking so much. Go enjoy your night with your not-fiancé and stop thinking about it."

"Easier said than done."

"Goodnight, Brynn," Emma sang and hung up. I stared at the black screen of my phone for a minute then stood up and took off my makeup. When I walked into the bedroom, Luke was shirtless and watching the end of a game.

My eyes darted to the drawer where I'd found the ring in before I slipped between the covers next to Luke. He put out his arm to signal he wanted me to come closer and I did. I leaned my head against his warm chest and sighed as I got into a comfortable position.

Doing this every night for the last few months had been wonderful. It'd been perfect even. Luke was someone I loved so much it hurt. He could have died from being shot and I wasn't chancing leaving his side again.

He had taken the right step towards getting me comfortable with marriage by asking me to move in. That seemed like the right move for us, and it didn't scare me at all.

Maybe he was going to wait until the right time. It was kind of sweet that he'd purchased something early on in anticipation of wanting to marry me.

"I can hear you thinking, Brynn," Luke cooed as he switched off the TV and looked down at me. He brushed my hair from my cheek and his expression was peaceful.

"I was thinking of moving in," I said quietly, even though it was a lie.

"And?" he prodded.

"I want the spare room closet."

He laughed and his chest almost shook me off him. I couldn't help my smile back at that.

"What? It's the biggest one and it's a walk-in!" I argued.

"Okay, it's yours," he said.

"Can I decorate how I want?"

He sighed, but his smile never left. "Yes, but nothing too floral."

"Deal."

I was glad I hadn't purchased Emma's house. I just had to get over my fear of commitment and even though it was taking me a little bit of time, I was happy to move in.

I laid back down on his chest and wrapped my arm around him. He flipped off the light and kissed my head as I closed my eyes.

He wasn't rushing me, he was taking his time. Maybe the ring wasn't what I thought.

Just as I was about to fall asleep, Luke said quietly, “I was thinking we’d go to the summer festival next weekend.”

I opened my eyes. “Really?”

“Yeah, it might be fun.”

Shit. Was that going to be the night he proposed?

Chapter Eight

A Festival of Disappointments

That week I felt like I was walking on eggshells. I was nervous and fidgety, and Emma thought it was hilarious.

"A lot of people get engaged at the summer festival. It's romantic and fun!"

"You're not helping," I muttered as I dressed a mannequin to put in the window.

"Sam and I were planning to go, we could meet up with you," she suggested.

"No, because I don't want anyone there when we get engaged."

"Brynn Clark," she snapped. "Are you going to say no?"

"Probably not! But I don't know!" I retorted, tightening the shirt on the mannequin. "I'm not ready to answer that question much less be proposed to again."

Mackayla walked in and heard the tail end of the conversation and stopped with a raised brow. "Are we talking about Brynn and her commitment issues again?"

"Yes!" Emma said at the same time I said no.

Mackayla just grinned. "Listen, Brynn, all the single ladies in Cold Spring have their eyes on Luke so if you don't make him your husband soon, someone is going to swoop in and steal him!"

I stiffened, the last part hit a little too close to home and Mackayla and Emma saw. I looked back at the mannequin and paused a few moments.

"I didn't keep the first one happy, how am I supposed to make sure Luke doesn't cheat on me either?"

"Brynn, that's not what she meant," Emma said with a sad sigh.

"I'm sorry, it was insensitive of me. I didn't mean it," Mackayla responded.

I stepped back from the window and crossed my arms. "I don't know how I can keep Luke."

Emma walked over and took my hand in hers. "Be yourself and be honest with him. That's how you'll keep him."

On the day of the summer festival, I came home from work and found Luke already dressed and ready. Automatically I looked at both of the pockets in his cargo shorts to check for lumps and bumps. I didn't see any.

"Hey sweetie," he said and swooped over to kiss me gently. "Did you have a good day at work?"

Had Owen ever really asked me that and meant it? Maybe, but even when I did respond, he hadn't listened.

"Not very eventful but I did miss you," I said, leaning closer to wrap my arms around him. He liked that answer and gave me a slow, lengthy kiss that had me thinking of things other than the festival.

"Why don't we stay home tonight?" I whispered, breaking away to kiss his neck.

His chuckle was manly and deep. "As much as I like the idea of that, I haven't gone to a summer festival before."

"It's the same as any dumb festival," I muttered, pulling back to look at him.

"We'll only go for a little bit, then we'll come back," he suggested, seeming pushy.

“O-Okay,” I stuttered, swallowing hard.

“Dress in something cute,” he said leaning down to playfully nip my bottom lip.

“Cute?”

I did as he requested and picked a little floral dress that had tiny blue flowers all over it. It was more Emma’s style than mine, but she’d convinced me I needed it because it looked good.

I grabbed a sweater in case I got cold, and we left the house. Luke kept his hand on my leg the entire drive to the festival. He was smiling over at me and all I could do was give an awkward, nervous smile back.

"I love you," he said softly, and I took in a quiet breath and repeated it back.

He didn't have a ring box in his pockets...Maybe he'd taken the ring out of the box?

"I heard they'll have fireworks after dark tonight," Luke mentioned. "We can stay for that then head home."

"Okay."

He glanced over, seeming concerned. "Are you okay, Brynn? You seem nervous?"

"I'm fine. Just worried about seeing a lot of people I know," I muttered.

He chuckled. "You'll be fine, you have me."

I did have Luke.

And he was also the Luke that was possibly proposing.

Proposing.

I was going to marry Luke.

Whoa, did this divorcee just come to terms with getting remarried?

Not really, but the thought did settle my stomach just a tad.

This was Luke. Not another Owen or anyone else. It was *Luke.*

The summer festival was packed with people from all over the county. Carnival rides flashed with bright colors and the screams of joyous and frightened patrons rang as we walked in.

It reminded me of my childhood when Mark would bring Dylan and me to the festival. I spent time trying to win a goldfish that would surely die the following day while Dylan would get caught for doing something illegal and Mark had been making out with Emma by the lake.

The memories made me open my phone and send a quick text to our sibling chat.

Me: *Summer Festival hasn't changed since we were kids. Pretty sure all the*

rides are the same from when we came. Which means they are still dangerous.

Mark: *That's why we haven't taken Bailey and Aaron. Not chancing a trip to the ER and a lawsuit.*

Lauren: *Isn't that where Dylan set a cart on fire and was taken to jail for the night?*

Dylan: *Good times, good times*

I snorted, thinking of the memory as Luke held my free hand as we walked together.

"Officer Price!" a man called out.

We turned on our heels and Luke smiled as he said, "David."

David was an older man with a bald head, and I recognized him as the chief of the fire department.

"How are you feeling? You've been in our thoughts and prayers," David said nicely.

"I'm almost healed up. I had Brynn take care of me," Luke pulled me to his side and planted a kiss on my head.

David smiled. "That's good. You take care of him, Brynn. God knows someone has to!" he joked. "Well, I'll let you love birds go. Tonight is a special night I'm sure." He winked at me and then waved as he walked away.

A special night?

My stomach twisted.

"What'd he mean by that?" I asked as we started walking again. Luke didn't look at me but I watched him reach into his left pocket.

"Who the hell knows? David is an odd one," Luke said but my eyes were trained on his hand. After a second, he pulled his hand out empty.

It was in there. It had to be in there. Box or not, it was in there.

I took a deep breath and summoned all the courage I could find, took his hand, and we walked to the food truck area.

We met up with Emma and Sam after we stuffed our faces with chicken fingers and fries and fried Oreos for dessert.

Emma latched onto my arm as Sam and Luke chatted about something ahead of us.

"Did he do it yet?" She whispered.

"No, and the longer he waits, the more anxious I get!" I complained.

She giggled. "You're a mess, Brynn!"

"I am well aware of that."

The fireworks started and my stomach twisted again. I realized it might have also been all the fried food but when Luke's arms came over my shoulders to pull me back into him, I confirmed it was definitely nerves.

Everyone stopped what they were doing and watched the lights flash against the night sky. Oohs and ahhs were heard and the field around us filled up with people. Then I looked out and saw Mackayla with her boyfriend. Suddenly Darren dropped to one knee and Mackayla's screech was heard by everyone as she yelled out 'yes!"

Luke chuckled and clapped as everyone else did.

I waited.

And waited.

And waited.

But Luke did nothing. He put his arms back around me and hugged me, putting his cheek against mine. After the big fireworks finale, he pulled away from me and started talking to Sam about where and who was setting off the fireworks.

I looked at Emma who seemed just as confused and shrugged.

Why hadn't he proposed? Tonight would have been the perfect time.

"You ready to go?" Luke asked.

I didn't answer, I nodded my head, and we got back to the truck and he opened the door for me to climb in.

I sat there, seeming confused and even frustrated.

Why hadn't he done it? What was he waiting for?

I was quiet the whole ride home and of course Luke noticed. He reached across and put his hand on my leg, much like he'd always done.

"You're quiet," he commented.

"I'm thinking."

"About what?"

"Nothing."

He sighed deeply at that. He hated when I didn't explain, but what was I supposed to say?

I'm annoyed because you didn't pop the question? Because I had prepared myself for this night and to say yes but then you never proposed?

The closer we got to the house, the more frustrated I grew.

When we finally pulled up in front of the house Luke turned to me.

"Clark, I'm not going to play twenty questions so spit it out."

I wanted to clap my mouth shut to keep word vomit from spilling out but even my hand wouldn't work.

"I thought you were going to propose to me tonight!" It sounded like I was yelling at him, and my outburst even scared me.

Luke didn't jump though, but I felt my face flame with embarrassment. When I got the courage to look at him, I saw his confused expression.

"Propose?" he repeated like it was a foreign word he hadn't heard before.

"Yes. Propose."

"Like ask you to marry me?"

"Yes."

His eyes grew big and my embarrassment worsened. He hadn't even been considering it! I could see it on his face.

But what about the damn ring? How could he be this surprised when he bought a ring?

"Why would you think that?"

I closed my eyes and took a breath.

Just spit it out Brynn.

"I found a ring in your top right drawer."

His eyebrows pushed together. "A ring?"

"Yes! I wasn't snooping or anything. I was putting away your shirts from the laundry and I found the ring. I thought you'd do it soon and you've been acting weird—"

"*I've* been acting weird?" he snapped. "*I've* been acting fine. You on the other hand haven't."

I glared. "It's because I thought you were going to propose!"

"I don't even understand what ring you're—" He stopped mid-sentence and I saw recognition fall across his expression. He put his thumb and forefinger across the bridge of his nose, closed his eyes, and sighed. "The one in the blue box?"

"Yes! See! You do know what I'm talking about!"

He dropped his hand and opened his eyes and glared back at me. "It's Emma's ring, Brynn. Sam asked me to hold it for him since it's supposed to be a surprise on their wedding day. It isn't yours."

Oh God. Emma's ring? It was hers? *Shit.*

He saw my expression and looked disappointed in me. "You told Emma about the ring, didn't you?"

"She's my best friend, Luke! I tell her everything! How was I supposed to know it was hers?" I defended myself but felt the weight of guilt fall on me.

I'd told her about her own ring! I'd ruined that secret for them. All because I was so worried about getting remarried.

"Brynn," Luke said in frustration. He got out of the truck and I did too, following behind him.

"What was I supposed to think? You had a nice dinner for me the other night when I came home from work. Then you invite me to the summer festival and act all weird and you've been fiddling in your pocket so much tonight!"

He stopped on the porch and turned to look at me as if I was clinically insane. "I did all those things because I wanted to spend time with you."

"Then what's in your pocket?" I demanded, crossing my arms stubbornly.

He pulled out the lining in his pockets to show nothing. "I have a bug bite on my leg from fishing the other day, Brynn. I am scratching it without being obvious!"

I slowly uncrossed my arms, feeling ridiculously stupid. My face flamed with embarrassment. "Oh."

He unlocked the house and walked in and I stood on the porch still trying to comprehend everything.

He had no ring in his pocket...it was a bug bite.... a freaking bug bite!

I was an idiot. Might as well put a sign around my neck and throw me in the town square.

I finally walked in as Luke went to the fridge to grab a beer. He cracked open the top and threw back a big swallow. Felix came down the steps and paced between our legs trying to get attention.

My cheeks still felt hot and I wanted to disappear into the walls. I stared at Luke, wondering if I'd made a mistake by telling him this. I didn't want him to know how insane I was and this definitely didn't help.

Looking straight ahead and not at me, Luke started, "If I would have proposed, what would you have said?" His eyes connected with mine.

I paused, my heart leaping a little at his question. I wanted to give him the real, Brynn answer. Not something made up.

"I would have said yes." Even I was surprised by how confident I sounded and how sincere it was.

Was I serious? Would I have actually said yes?

"You're ready for that?" he questioned, his eyes narrowing.

I squirmed under his hard gaze. "I think."

He scoffed and took another sip of beer. "If I propose, it's a one-time shot, Brynn," he said with seriousness. His brown eyes showed hurt and a little anger. "If the answer is no, there won't be another chance to say yes."

When his first girlfriend told him no when he proposed, he was heartbroken, embarrassed, and upset.

"I want to make sure when it does get asked, that we both are on the same page. There can be no doubt in either of us that this is the next step."

I nodded, not trusting my words.

He wasn't going to propose. That's what this conversation had told me. It wasn't happening anytime soon. Part of me was disappointed and the other part was relieved. I really was messed up. Emma was right, a therapist was a good idea.

Not trying to show my true feelings, I mumbled, "I'm going to go up and change,"

He watched me walk up the stairs with Felix in tow. I went to the bathroom to change out of my dress and slip on my shorts and t-shirt. I looked at myself in the mirror and couldn't believe I had tears shining in my eyes.

Disappointed tears? Relieved tears? What was it?

If I wanted to get married, I had to show him that I was ready. Whether I really was or not, it was time to show my commitment to him.

I couldn't be upset that he didn't propose when I wasn't giving a full hundred percent to our relationship. It was time; I had to give my all. That meant officially moving in and not pushing it off anymore.

When I went downstairs, he was staring out the kitchen window, almost finished with his beer. He glanced at me and seemed surprised I came back down.

"I think next month is a good time to start moving my stuff in," I casually said, reaching around him to get a bottle of water from the fridge.

He raised a curious brow. "Next month?"

"Yes."

He still watched me with those police eyes that intimidated me and made me excited at the same time. I stepped closer to him until he was forced to put an arm around me and let me lean into him. “I want to be here with you, in this house, together.”

He pushed my hair off my shoulder and then leaned down to kiss me slowly.

A meow reached our ears as Felix watched us as he sat beside his empty food bowl.

Chapter Nine

We Go at Our Pace

I moved in with Luke at the end of August and we decided to have a family dinner to invite everyone to the house.

We set up two picnic tables in the backyard and Luke grilled with Dylan and Mark standing around talking about the football season starting.

Mom and Dad came around from the front yard with Bill walking beside him. Barney skidded around the corner and jumped on Dylan almost knocking him to the ground. He cursed loudly and Kate just barely got hands over Aaron's ears but not Bailey's. She giggled and smacked his arm.

"Uncle Dylan, you aren't allowed to say that word."

Mark glared daggers. "Yeah, not a word to say around my kids."

Dylan, still cupping his groin, said, "I'm sorry but Luke, your dad's dog is gonna be next on the grill if it ball taps me again."

Luke flinched. "Dad! Control Barney please!" he snapped.

Kate and Lauren helped me set the table with plastic cups and plates.

"So," Lauren said quietly. "Is he going to propose now?"

I paused and looked at her, Kate glanced up curious to hear too. "I don't know to be honest. Moving in together is our first step and a big one at that," I explained quietly.

"There's no rush," Kate said. "Take the time to get to know each other before taking that leap again."

"Definitely," I agreed. "I don't think I'm ready just yet…soon though."

Lauren just grinned. "I'm dying to help plan another wedding again so keep me updated!"

I rolled my eyes as Mom came over and slipped her arm around my waist.

"Hello, my girls, what are we talking about?"

"Men," Lauren said.

"Sorry, I can't give advice to you two on that. You're the ones who got suckered into this family," Mom said jokingly.

"It's a good family to get suckered into," Kate explained with a small smile.

Mom looked thrilled. "Maybe we can get that one into it too, what do you say, Brynn?" Mom pointed towards Luke manning the grill with all the men around him.

"One day maybe, but not yet," I said quietly.

We sat down at the table with hot dogs and hamburgers and plenty of side dishes to go around. Luke sat next to me and put his arm around my shoulders.

"Thanks for coming today," Luke announced to the table. "We appreciate you helping Brynn move into our place and celebrating it with us."

"I'm not moving any more damn couches," Dad muttered loud enough for most of us to hear and for Mom to elbow him in the stomach.

"Just take care of our sis, that's all we ask," Mark piped up with a smile toward Luke.

"No problem there," Luke responded.

Beer glasses clinked and the kids knocked their soda cans as Barney sat very close to Aaron by the table. He knew who the messiest eater was.

Just like everything else in my life, Luke fit perfectly in it. He was everything I needed and, to my shock, what my family needed.

Luke leaned over and kissed my head and I laughed when Aaron tried to sneak a hotdog below the table to give to Barney.

"Damn dog," Luke muttered. "We're definitely not getting one."

I shook my head at him. "They're not all like that."

He just chuckled as his dad dragged Barney from under the table and made him sit beside him. He whined and barked at being pulled away from a possible meal.

"So, what's next with you two?" Mark asked, taking a bite of his burger.

Luke's and my head whipped around so quickly I thought we'd both suffered whiplash.

"What do you mean?" I asked. Kate's cheeks turned red and she mouthed a 'sorry' to us.

"I mean," he said, swallowing his bite and looking all but the dad he was. "Are you guys thinking of more commitment?"

I heard Lauren whispering something to Dylan and he choked on his hamburger. "What?" he tried to be quiet.

"I think—" Before I could say anything Lauren came to my rescue.

"Sorry to interrupt but Dylan and I have news," she announced.

"Ah shit, now?" Dylan muttered to her.

Everyone paused to look at the two of them.

Lauren's face glowed with happiness and Dylan finally put down his burger and threw an arm around her shoulder.

"Everyone, we're expecting a baby," Dylan said loudly.

Mom was the first to squeal and jump from the table, Dad looked proud and Mark and Kate got up to hug them.

Luke looked stunned and happy and we all took turns congratulating them.

"How far along are you?" Mom asked, wiping tears from her eyes.

Lauren, holding a hand across her stomach grinned. “Three months. We’re due in February!”

“You sure you’re ready to be a dad?” Mark asked, patting Dylan on the back.

“I think it’s coming no matter what I do,” he said with a chuckle.

“You’ll do great, man, congratulations.” Luke gave him a hug.

We sat back down as the kids dove into their dessert which were ice cream bars. Kate leaned across the table with eyes so bright and happy.

“I have so many baby clothes! Both genders so don’t buy too much until you’ve looked through what I have. Oh my gosh! There are these amazing books—"

Luke put his arm back around me and kissed my head again as I watched my sisters-in-law bond over my newest niece or nephew on the way. A pang of.... jealousy? Or like I was the odd one out because I didn’t have that yet?

“How’s your morning sickness? I know this company that sells ginger lollipops that really do the trick!” Kate exclaimed.

“Yes, please! I’ve been throwing up every morning at 6 am on the dot!” Lauren responded.

I smiled at the conversation but again, I didn’t understand. Owen and I had never tried to have kids, though it was part of the plan. A plan that was thankfully derailed.

I looked at Luke who was conversing with my father across the table as my mother joined my sisters-in-law in conversation about morning sickness remedies.

They were in a different part of their life than me. I was…behind. Divorce had pushed back my world and I had to start from scratch again. I would be thirty next year…one step closer to my childbearing years being over.

Screw Pam Rally for even putting that shit in my head. I wouldn't let that get to me. I couldn't.

I straightened a little and turned towards the boys having a debate on which football team would be the most successful this year and listened to that.

When I crawled into bed that night with Luke, I was exhausted. We'd had a fun day together as a family with the news of a new little one and our moving-in together.

Luke kissed my head as I got comfortable on his shoulder.

He turned the TV on to a late-night show and I watched it without really seeing it.

"Do you want kids?" I asked quietly.

"Sure, eventually," Luke said, his voice soft.

"I'm going to be thirty next year, Luke."

He pushed me back a little to look at me, his brows creasing. "Is this because of Lauren?"

I sat up on my knees and played with the material of the blanket. "Yes and no."

He sat up, leaning his back against the headboard. "Talk."

"I thought I'd be further along in my life by now," I mumbled. "Everyone expects me to jump right into marriage again and start having babies, but I can't...well, we can't because, you know, it takes two to do both of those things."

"I'm aware," he said with a smirk that made my insides melt a bit.

"I feel rushed... I feel like I should be doing more and it's getting to me."

Luke was quiet for a moment until I looked up into his eyes. His hand strayed to my cheek. "No one is rushing you, Brynn. If they are, they are the assholes. *We* make our own timeline; *we* make the choices *we* want. No one else has a say."

"But don't you feel like your life is ticking away and you feel like you're out of control?" I whispered.

He smiled softly and rubbed his thumb over my bottom lip. "No, Sweetheart, I don't. I feel like I found someone who helps me feel in control again."

How could a girl not love a man when he spoke like that?

"Just because other people are moving forward in their life doesn't mean you aren't. You're going the same pace but you're achieving things differently. No way is the right way. It's our way," Luke explained.

"Promise?"

He leaned up and tangled his hand in my hair. "Yes, I promise."

He kissed me and I drifted back into his embrace.

Months went by and Luke and I got into the rhythm of living together. Dinner every Friday night together was a must. Then Sulivan's on Saturdays with Emma and Sam. Sundays were the lazy days where we spent time with my family and even Bill came a few times.

We had a beautiful baby shower for Lauren that Kate, mom, and I put together. They were having a little girl and by the looks of the gifts and the turn out, she was already very loved.

It was now winter, and Thanksgiving came and went and we were only three weeks from Christmas.

Emma and I worked extra at Feather Blue and bought more inventory to handle the heavy shopping days ahead.

"Ew, this smells like an old lady perfume," Emma sniffed a black blouse that someone had tried on. I took it from her and almost gagged.

"Not to be weird but this smells like my ex-mother-in-law. Makes me want to get in the fetal position and recite name brands. Throw it in the dirty bin."

Emma laughed. "Was she that horrible?"

I walked over to put a few pieces of clothing away on a rack by the window. "Oh yes. If you look up Satan's Mistress in the dictionary, Pam Rally's name is right underneath it," I muttered.

"Well okay," Emma said, laughing harder. "I'm glad Sam's mom isn't like that. She's always been strict with her kids and had high expectations but she's really sweet and likes me."

I put the stuff away and walked back to her. "That's good because honestly, that makes or breaks a relationship." I chewed on my lip as Emma straightened a dress. "Did I tell you Pam came and saw me over the summer?"

Her head snapped up and her jaw dropped. "I'm about to disown you as my best friend! She did not!"

I nodded reluctantly. "It was right after Luke got shot so I only told my mom."

Emma was fully engaged with the conversation, dropping her task to listen.

"She wanted me to take Owen back," I finally spit out.

"Shut up! No way!" Emma exclaimed. "What'd you say?"

"Um, hell no! I told her she was crazy and sent her on her merry way."

Emma's shocked expression stayed on her face until she blinked. "Wow, I can't believe that. Do you think Owen would just show up here?"

I scoffed and printed a receipt from the register. "He'd be stupid to do so. If he knocked on Luke's door, he'll most likely pummel him into a small, preppy box."

"Our door," Emma corrected.

"Yes, *our* door."

We finished cleaning up the store and were about to head out when I looked at my calendar. "After the holidays, are we scheduling a girl's day to figure out some more wedding planning?" I asked her. I had to plan a bridal shower and a bachelorette party so that meant I needed to get things figured out asap.

"Yes! I'm thinking a day in January," she concluded.

"You got it, future Mrs. Locklear!"

We waved our goodbyes and I got into my car and drove down the road. The winter had picked up and the cold wind blew my car around. I white knuckled the steering wheel to stay on the road. I drove along the Hudson, leaning forward trying to make sure there weren't any deer in the road but in this cold weather, they'd probably be hunkered down, staying warm.

Suddenly, something ran out in front of me, and I slammed on my brakes hard to swerve and miss the animal. As I did, I caught sight of what it was. It was a dog!

Chapter Ten

Molly

My car came to a halt, just missing the animal and my heartbeat heavily against my chest as I stared at the black and white dog on the side of the road. Its tail was tucked between its legs and was shaking. As it stared at me, I wasn't sure if it was shaking for fear of almost being killed or from the cold. I checked my review mirror and saw no one coming and got out of my car.

The dog seemed frozen in fear as it saw me come around the car to talk to it.

"Hi puppy, I'm not going to hurt you. You shouldn't be out here, you'll freeze to death."

It still didn't move. Half of its face was black and the other side white with one green and one brown eye. Its black and white coat was matted and I couldn't see a collar.

I could very well get bit and have to get a rabies shot for what I was about to do. I crouched down and stretched out my hand. "Come here," I whispered encouragingly.

Its tail moved slightly then it put its head down and slowly walked to me. I was stunned as it came closer, lowering itself to the ground, tail only wagging a little. It came in under my hand and the fur was matted and dirty.

"It's okay," I said quietly, petting its head. I looked under its legs and saw it was a female.

"Girl, you're a girl," I said, more to myself than to the dog.

A car beeped its horn as it drove past. The dog jumped up and almost ran, but I touched her gently and tried to keep her close. I needed to get her in the car.

Would she get in the car?

I stood up slowly and went to my back passenger side door, but the dog had backed up a little.

"Come here, girl. Come with me, I'll keep you warm."

She didn't hesitate anymore but ran and leaped into the backseat as I stood there shocked. She curled up in the corner and her tail wagged slightly with her head bowed.

Had she been abused?

I shut the door quietly, not wanting to spook her, and ran to the front seat. I turned up the heat and drove down the road slowly. I pulled out my phone and glanced in the back. The dog was still curled up, not moving much.

Was she starved? Did someone lose her?

I dialed Luke's number and bit my lip.

"Everything okay?" he answered automatically.

"Yes...."

"Brynn?" He rarely used my name anymore, so I knew he was suspicious.

"Don't kill me okay—"

"I already don't like the start of this—"

"There was a dog—"

"Absolutely not. We aren't getting a dog."

"What if it just jumped into the back of my car?"

He scoffed. "I damn well know that didn't happen."

I pulled into the driveway and turned off my lights. "What if it did? Luke, she was out wandering on the road by the Hudson. I almost hit her. She's starved and scared and cold. I couldn’t leave her there."

He sighed and growled at the same time, and I saw him look out the door.

"You've got to be kidding me."

"Listen, do you have one of Barney's leashes? I'm afraid she'll be too spooked to come inside. If she's someone's dog I don't want her to run away."

"Hold on," he muttered.

A few seconds later, he walked outside with a leash in his hands. I got out and looked in the back seat. She was still curled up, not moving. He looked in too and sighed louder.

“Brynn—”

“It’s temporary, Luke. This could be someone’s dog and they could be looking for her. It’s close to Christmas. Imagine losing your family dog right around there?"

He ran a hand over his mouth. "Fine. But if you get bit, I'm going to be the one to poke those shots into your ass."

I gently put the leash around her neck, and she stirred a little and started shaking again.

"Come on, girl, come with me."

She slowly exited the car and looked at Luke with a little fear and knocked into my legs, hiding from him. I petted her head and encouraged her to come up the stairs and into the house.

"She looks rough, Sweetheart," Luke mumbled, a strain to his voice.

"I know, it's why I had to get her."

The border collie hesitantly walked into the house and Luke shut the door slowly and shrugged off his jacket then helped me take off mine.

She put her nose in the air and sniffed around then when I took the leash off, she padded over to the rug in front of the unlit fireplace and curled up. As if this was always her home and she felt comfortable.

I glanced at Luke who was frowning at the scene as if shocked by it too.

"I'll light it," he said with a sigh. The dog perked up as he knelt down close to her by the fireplace. Her tail wagged hard on the floor and he barely paid her any mind as the flames lit the logs and the room started to warm.

I went to the kitchen and filled a bowl with water and grabbed some cheese cubes from the fridge. I sat down on the floor in front of her and offered the water.

She gladly lapped at it, and I felt my heart tighten at how thirsty she was. She ate all the cheese cubes from my hand and was very gentle, not vicious or mean or even nippy.

When I looked up at Luke he was sitting on the edge of the couch, his eyes furrowed, watching us.

"I can't tell if she's just a sweet, calm dog or if she's sick," I said, my voice cracking a little.

"I don't know. How will Felix react until we find the owner?"

I looked toward the stairs where I thought he'd be sitting waiting for attention, but he was nowhere to be found. Probably watching and sniffing from afar.

"I'm not sure. I don't know how he'll be with a dog. We can put a chair in front of the stairs so she stays down here and Felix can get away," I offered as a solution.

I stood up slowly and the border collie sighed heavily and put her head on her paws and closed her eyes. I sat down beside Luke on the couch and we both just stared at her matted fur. The white mixed with the black looked closer to brown.

"I'm sorry, Luke. I couldn't leave her out there. Tonight is supposed to be down below zero—"

He put his hand on my knee and patted. “It’s fine. I know why you did it.”

I gave him a relieved smile and kissed him. “I need to go out and get some dog food. I’ll call the vet and leave a message to see if they can get her in tomorrow to check for a microchip.”

The thought of finding her home made me secretly hope she didn’t have one. She seemed content here with us and I felt content having her here.

“I wonder what her name is,” I whispered.

“She had no collar?”

I shook my head no. “It doesn’t even look as if she ever had one.”

She opened her eyes and looked at us, barely moving her head, as if she trusted us not to hurt her.

I already wanted to keep her.

I rushed to the store that night and got dog food, puppy pads in case she wasn’t potty trained, a leash and harness, and, of course, toys and treats. I got home within an hour and when I walked in the door with all the bags, Luke was sitting on the floor, the border collie was stretched over his lap. He was petting her slowly with a quirk on his lips. She lifted her head as I walked in and I saw her expression light up, as if she remembered who I was.

She got up and came over to me slowly, her head bowed but her tail wagging.

"Hi girl, were you being good?" I cooed.

"She's been sleeping," Luke said, standing up and brushing the hair off his legs.

I smirked at him. "For a man who doesn't like dogs, you seemed very comfortable on the floor with her."

He shrugged and started looking through the bags. We watched her go and drink from the bowl in the kitchen, surprised at how easily she was adjusting.

"I got a few things to help in case she's like Barney."

I pulled out toys and the bag of dog food and I even bought bigger bowls for her. I put some kibble into the bowl and she came over to stand and wagged her tail harder as she saw what I had.

"Let me feed her in case she's starving and tries to bite."

I handed Luke the bowl and he put a hand up to the dog to wait. After placing it on the floor, he said the magic word, *okay,* and she dove in, her tail still wagging as she devoured the food.

We watched her finish her bowl and she happily looked up at us for more. We knew not to overfeed her so it wouldn't make her sick.

She went to the door suddenly, whimpered, and paced. It was then I realized she had to go to the bathroom. I quickly got her leash on and took her outside where she did her business while Luke watched on the porch. Within a few minutes, she was shivering and bolted right back inside without me having to drag her in. I took off her leash and she went over to the fireplace and curled up right where she had been before.

Luke and I stared in amazement. She seemed like a good dog, unlike crazy-head Barney.

We sat down together on the couch and Luke nestled me in under his arm as we watched her.

"I'm going to give her a bath tomorrow. I don't think she has fleas, but I think I should make sure and get her coat brushed out."

"I'll call Chris Rhodes from Long Rhodes Ahead Animal Rescue and see if they are missing a dog," Luke suggested. "If they don't know her, I'll ask around town."

The Rhodes family were good people. Gemma and Keith and their son, Chris, had started the rescue years and years ago when they saw a need. They were good at keeping tabs on rescues though so I couldn't imagine they had one get loose.

"If we knew her name–"

"Don't be naming her," Luke muttered.

I rolled my eyes. "What do we call her then? Dog? Hey You?"

He pinched the bridge of his nose. "You're going to be the death of me."

I scoffed. "That's a little dramatic."

"Fine, call her whatever, but do not get attached, Brynn. She probably has a home."

I smiled at my victory and moved to set down beside her. Her tail banged against the floor. She rolled onto her back and let me scratch her belly.

I rattled off a few dog names, but none affected her. She still laid there, enjoying the scratches. I stopped and leaned back on the couch and touched Luke's leg.

"What does she even look like to you?" I prodded. I didn't think he'd give me an answer, as she rolled over and sat up in front of us, putting her head in Luke's lap. Her bicolored eyes looked into his and I saw him melt.

Sucker.

"Molly," he said, and I raised a surprised brow.

Her tail hit the floor and she shifted excitedly, and my mouth dropped open in surprise.

"Molly?" I repeated and she looked at me, her head tilting and ears perking up.

I petted her as she settled down in front of us and Luke sighed.

"Don't forget to call the vet," he remarked, and I smiled to myself.

We put away everything that she could get into, and I even hid the new pillows from the couch just in case. Felix was still nowhere to be found but we headed up to bed. The next morning, I woke quickly and ran down the stairs to check on Molly. When I stepped into the living room, I was very surprised to see her still curled up on the rug and Felix laying on the couch curled up too. They were only a few feet from each other.

Whoa, were they actually getting along?

"Molly?" I said softly and her head snapped up. She wagged her tail and stretched before coming over to greet me. Felix made a meowing sound but that didn't trigger Molly or anything. I took her outside to go to the bathroom and as soon as she was done, she half dragged me back in.

As I fed her breakfast, Dr. McCauslin called and scheduled Molly for their first visit of the day. I got myself ready and Luke got up and met me downstairs when I was about to take her.

"How'd she do?"

"She didn't touch a thing last night," I said quietly.

She was back on the rug in front of the fireplace and Felix was stretching and jumping off the couch. We watched with our breaths held tightly as he went over to Molly. She sniffed him and pushed him around with her nose but then sighed and put her head down to rest. Felix purred and rubbed onto her and flopped down on his side against her.

Luke's jaw dropped and my heart did little jumps at the sight of their friendship.

"Molly, come on girl." She lifted her head but didn't look at all like she wanted to go anywhere today.

I couldn't blame her.

I got her to the vet with some pushing because she didn't like getting in the car. Though she settled once we got on the road, I saw her visibly shaking so I tried to crank up the heat.

When we arrived, Skyler met us in one of the exam rooms. She was short with blonde, almost golden hair always tucked into a clip of some sort. She was a few years younger than me, but I remembered her being a nice girl in high school.

"Where did you say you found her?"

"By the Hudson, close to our house. She was just wandering on the road, and seemed so sad," I expressed as I saw her tail tucked.

"She's not in thc greatest of shape. She's a little dehydrated and skinny, so food, water, and some vitamins should help. We'll treat her for heartworms too," the vet said.

"Do you know anyone missing their family dog?"

Skyler pulled back from listening to Molly's heart and shook her head. "Not a border collie mix. Other dogs, yes, but she isn't one I recognize. Let me check for a chip." She grabbed a scanner from a drawer and hovered it over Molly's neck.

She shook her head. "No chip. Did you guys call in and talk to Gemma or Chris Rhodes yet?"

"Luke was going to do that today."

Molly turned and licked Skyler's hand. It broke my heart a moment thinking she had to have a family. "Do you know how old she is?"

Skyler gently inspected her teeth then brushed back her head and gave her scratches. All the while Molly did so well, never biting or growling.

"From the looks of the teeth, she's barely two. She could have been from one of the puppy mills someone dropped off along the highway. Unfortunately, that happens more than I'd like to know," she explained, her eyes hardening. "She needs some flea and tick meds and put on a special diet to get her weight up and she'll be better than ever. Also…a bath." Molly sat up and looked at me, her eyes shining two different colors.

"Can you keep an eye out for anyone that might be missing her? As much as I'd love to keep her, Luke and I don't want to keep someone's family dog."

And Luke might kill me if I come back without a solution.

She smiled kindly. "Yes, when anyone brings in a dog they've found, we post fliers around town and on social media. We keep them up for 90 days. If no one comes to collect her, you can bring her back in and we work with Gemma to get her a home or you can keep her," Skyler said.

I nodded and sighed, putting the leash back over Molly's neck. "Thank you for all your help, Dr. McCauslin. We appreciate it."

Molly seemed much better once we got back to the house and she went storming in to sit by the fireplace again.

I still had a little time before work and decided to give her a bath. The hardest part was getting her upstairs. She was scared of them and whined when I tried to encourage her to come up. Eventually, I put her on the leash and drug her. Halfway up, she got comfortable and ran the rest of the way. I got her into the bathroom and shut the door.

I pointed to the shower curtain and rug and narrowed my eyes.

"If you eat either of these, you'll be going back for adoption."

As if she understood, her head bowed.

I got her into the tub easily to my surprise and as soon as the water turned on, she was biting at it.

I laughed and was glad she wasn't traumatized.

She came out clean and the tub had brown dirty water mulling within. Her white fur was beautiful, and she was extra soft from the dog shampoo Skyler gave me.

After her bath, I took a picture of her and sent it to my sibling group chat.

Me: *Meet Molly*

Lauren: *You convinced Luke to get a dog?!*

Me: *Not exactly. I found her along the road last night. We're taking care of her until we hear if she has a home.*

Dylan: *A stray maybe?*

Mark: *Different eyes. Hope she's not like Barney.*

Kate: *The kids saw her picture now they are demanding to come over to Aunt Brynnie's house.*

By one, she was drying in the living room, and I was rushing out of the house so I wouldn't be late for work.

I texted Luke on my way to tell him she was bathed and relaxing, and that the vet couldn't find a chip but would let us know if they found her home. He responded with a very Luke comment.

Okay.

I got to work only five minutes late, but the store was dead. Mackayla looked bored, leaning over the register and reading a wedding magazine.

"Hey, is Em in the back?" I asked.

She nodded. "Do you think I should do a black wedding dress? I've never been a traditional kind of girl," she said, actually looking for me to answer.

I paused on my retreat to the back. "Your mother would kill you," I responded.

She grinned. "I'm definitely wearing a black dress!"

I chuckled at her as I went to the backroom. Emma was on the phone with one of our suppliers asking for a shipment refill.

"I know you don't have any in stock but we don't either. I've just asked that when you get them in, you expedite a few boxes my way. I'll pay the extra for shipping costs. Okay, great! You're the best, Pat!" She hung up and looked at me with a triumphant smile.

"Does Pat know you have a future husband or are we just trying to get our way?" I mused, setting my purse down.

"*She* is quite nice and is willing to work something out for us to get those necklace sets in before Christmas."

We chuckled. I sat down at my desk and booted up my computer.

"You're not going to believe what happened to me last night," I started.

"Luke finally proposed?"

I rolled my eyes and glared at her. "No, but thanks for the reminder. I found a dog along the Hudson."

Emma's mouth dropped open in surprise. “Seriously?”

“Yes, she’s a collie mix. She was dirty and matted and just jumped into my car when I opened the door. We’re trying to find who she belongs to because she’s too sweet to be a stray,” I said.

“How’d Luke take to a dog in the house? I know Barney didn’t set a good reputation,” she winced.

“Surprisingly well. He let me name her Molly. But I can tell he wants to find her home quickly.”

“What if you can’t locate her home?” Emma waited for my response as I mulled it over.

“If I can convince him to keep her, I will. But I think it’s going to take a lot to do that,” I finally answered.

I was wrong. It probably wouldn’t take a lot of convincing.

When I arrived home that night, there was a large, fluffy bed sitting on top of that rug by the fireplace and Molly was happily sleeping on it. She woke up when I came in and came running to me with her tail wagging and head bowed, much how she’d done the night I’d found her.

"Hi girly," I said as I dropped to my knees to pet her. She licked my face, and I brushed my hands through her soft fur.

I looked up to see Luke putting food on two plates. He looked innocent as I straightened and put my stuff down.

"A bed?"

"Yeah, a rug isn't comfortable."

I couldn't help my smile. "Next thing you know you'll be letting her on the couch or the—"

"Absolutely not. No couch, no bed, and no truck," he snapped.

I just bit my lip with amusement as I slipped over to kiss him. Felix came running from over on the couch and sat next to Molly who stared up at us. I looked at the two of them, so strange that they'd get along so quickly, and realized what they wanted: food.

After dinner, we sat on the sofa together and watched a TV show. I leaned up against Luke with his warm arm around me. I glanced at Felix and Molly and prayed I could keep this.

As if on cue, my phone rang and I answered it quickly.

"This is Brynn."

"Hi Brynn, this is Chris from Long Rhodes Ahead Animal Rescue," Chris Rhodes said in his familiar deep voice. He'd been several years younger than me but had taken to working right alongside his parents with their amazing rescue. He was calling after I requested a phone call about Molly. My heart sputtered at that.

"Did Dr. McCauslin give you a description of Molly?" I asked, quietly.

"Sure did. After looking into it, she was never our rescue, and we have no missing border collies on our list. Unfortunately, we get a lot of drop offs, and this time of year is normally higher than others. We'll keep her in the database for about 90 days if someone would call in and report a missing collie. When those days are up, if you want to put her up for adoption, we can handle that for you."

I glanced at Luke who was just waiting, reading my expression. "Okay, sounds good. Thanks for getting back to us Chris."

"Anytime."

I hung up and just looked at Luke. "90 days?" he questioned with a sigh.

"Yeah…you okay with 90 days?"

He glanced at Molly who slept on her new bed quietly. She peeked open her eyes to look at us then rolled onto her back to display her stomach.

I chuckled and Luke cracked a smile.

"Fine," he said not so reluctantly.

Chapter Eleven

Loving You is Easy… Until I Check Your Phone

It was Christmas Eve when Luke seemed to have his mind off work and more on us. It was our first holiday together in his house.

Er, our house.

Emma would be annoyed by that.

I poured glasses of wine for us and curled up on the couch next to him as he turned on a Christmas movie.

I had decorated for Christmas by getting a small artificial tree and four stockings, though Luke made fun of me for getting one for Felix and Molly.

I still had hope that she would eventually be ours. I just had to convince Luke and pray no one came looking for her.

Luke had his arm around me, and I held onto him as I leaned my back against his chest. Molly sat on the floor in front of us, her head resting on Luke's leg as he petted her watching TV. He didn't even realize he was doing it. Felix sat behind me on the back of the couch.

"We should each open up one gift," I said. "Mom and Dad always let us open something from our stockings on Christmas Eve to get us all excited for the next morning."

Luke's smile was sweet, and I felt tingly all over. "Sure."

I was more excited for Molly's gift than anything and I quickly stood and went to her stocking. I pulled out the wrapped collar and got down on my knees to give it to her. She sniffed at it excitedly and I giggled when she nosed it open.

It was a purple collar with a tag that said "Molly" and gave our address and phone number. Luke leaned over to look closer at it.

Luke's brow was raised. "90 days?"

I knew by the tone of his voice he was wondering if I'd bought it right after finding Molly. I playfully glared. "Well, she does need something to hook her leash to so why not have one with her name on it?"

He shook his head and chuckled, but I didn't care. I put the collar around her neck, and she gladly waited, looking into my eyes, and her tail wagging loudly against the floor.

I kissed her head with a loud smacking sound, and she went over to see Luke.

Felix sat behind our heads along the back of the couch, just watching us.

"Tell her to go check her stocking," Luke said to Molly but then glanced at me.

I grinned and stood up to go check my stocking. There I found a small box. A ring box.

I felt my heart beating wildly against my chest as I turned around to look at Luke. He was smiling at me, but he hadn't moved from his seat on the couch.

What was he waiting for? He knew I saw the box?

I shakily pulled it out and saw a small red bow on the black velvet box. It had no indication of what brand it was or where it was from.

"Go ahead, you can open it," Luke encouraged.

I flipped the box open with a small pop and inhaled.

It wasn't an engagement ring but a beautiful set of diamond drop earrings. They were delicate and simple and probably would be the most expensive jewelry I would own. Even Owen, with all the money he had never bought me anything this nice.

"Wow," I said, trying not to let my voice show my disappointment. I wasn't disappointed with the earrings, they were beautiful, it was that they weren't an engagement ring.

Wow, I couldn't believe how my thoughts had changed from being so scared of commitment to badly wanting that commitment with Luke.

He finally stood up and came to loop his arms around me, his lips in a perfect smile. "I thought they'd looked beautiful on you. Do you like them?"

"Yes, of course," I expressed. "They look too expensive to even wear."

He chuckled and kissed me softly. "Wear them. Don't put them in the box and keep them tucked away. My mother did that for years and my father hated it. Jewelry is meant to be worn."

I took them out of the box and put them into my ears to show him they were going to get used. I pushed my hair back and moved my head from side to side.

"What do you think?"

"Beautiful," he whispered, leaning forward to kiss me deeply.

When we broke apart, I went to his stocking and pulled out one of his gifts trying to get over my disappointment. When I collected myself, I turned towards Luke and handed him his present. "It's definitely not diamond earrings," I mumbled, feeling bad that I hadn't gone that big.

He unwrapped the small box and opened it to find a black engraved pen.

I saw the astonishment in his expression.

Amor valet ad dolorem was etched on one side of the pen. It was the inscription his dad had quoted to his mother and when he turned it over another inscription was written.

"Amare tu est facilis," he said softly, his eyebrow creasing.

He looked up and I couldn't tell if he knew it or not. "Loving you is easy."

I saw his expression change from surprise to a soft, sweet look as he pulled me close and kissed me.

"Is this our quote?"

"Yes, until I get to the point where it isn't easy to love you."

He chuckled, his lips trailing over my earlobe, making a shiver run down my spine. "It'll come, just wait."

I smiled and took a deep breath when his kisses on my neck increased, and his hands tightened around my waist.

Gifts forgotten, thoughts forgotten, he gathered me in his arms, and we went upstairs together, leaving Molly and Felix by the fire.

On Christmas morning we exchanged our small gifts and had breakfast together. I didn't get an engagement ring in any of those gifts, but I tried to not let it bother me. He did get me a Glock pistol and he seemed really excited to show me how to use it. After we were done, he went upstairs to get a shower and left his phone on the kitchen counter.

I stared at it for a while, biting my thumbnail.

I shouldn't, I can't be that girl. The one who rifles through her boyfriend's phone. I just needed to see if he's been looking at engagement rings, that's it.

I put my coffee cup down and snuck over to his phone and turned it on. The screen lit up and it was a photo of Molly sitting in front of the fireplace. "I don't like dogs, my ass," I muttered.

The man barely ever changed the picture on his screen.

I swiped up and the keypad for the code appeared.

Shit, I hadn't thought of a code. We didn't share that stuff with each other because of the trust between us but now I wish I had.

His birthday.

Wrong.

Bill's birthday.

Wrong.

Mother's birthday.

Wrong.

My birthday.

Wrong.

I growled and shoved the phone back onto the counter in frustration. I had one more attempt before I got locked out.

Could it be our anniversary? I typed in the numbers and the home screen opened.

It *was our anniversary…how sweet. God but here I was being nosy as hell and snooping on his phone.*

I went to his browser history and found the website for Swan's Jewelry and my heart rate increased exceptionally.

Yes, yes!

But in his past purchases was a necklace and earring set. The earrings I'd opened last evening but not the necklace. He hadn't given that to me yet. The necklace was beautiful and the same silver as the earrings with the drop diamond pendant.

Maybe he'd gotten it for my mom for Christmas? I would find out this evening when we went there.

A text message came across the screen and it was Bill letting us know he was heading over. My parents had invited him for Christmas dinner since he normally spent the holidays with Luke. Mom felt empathy and wanted to make sure he was included.

I went to his text messages and right below Bill's message was a text from a number that wasn't saved in Luke's phone.

I clicked on it and opened up the conversation.

Let me know when she's gone. The person wrote.

I checked his call history and saw he'd made a phone call right after that text to that number. It had been sent two days ago in the morning after I'd left for work. Luke had off. He said he was going to wrap presents and take Molly on a walk.

My heart plummeted to my feet, and I felt cold all over. I read that text in a woman's voice.

Was she the one who got the necklace? Who was she?

I looked closely at the number, and it was a New York area code so it was definitely someone local.

The water shut off upstairs and I clicked off the apps I'd opened and put the phone down then I ran back over to the couch to sit and pretend I'd been there all along.

Luke came down shortly with a towel wrapped around his waist and his hair wet.

He grinned at me. "You aren't watching TV?" He looked at the black screen and seemed confused.

My heart was pounding hard in my chest. I didn't look at him when I answered.

"No, I'm just thinking."

He picked up his phone, came over to kiss me on the head, and went back upstairs.

"My dad's headed here," he called back down but I ignored him.

I had gone on his phone to find an engagement ring…not another woman. Was this my biggest fear? Finding the right man then finding out he was cheating? Just like Owen. Except, I never really knew Owen and had trusted him way too much. Luke couldn't be doing this to me. How could I think he was cheating on me? He loved me and practically begged me to live with him. I *felt* his love for me.

I had to be mistaken.

I stood up, planning to go upstairs to talk it out with him, but I stopped. I had been looking through his phone. That was not okay. He would be upset with me and say I betrayed his trust.

I groaned at my dilemma.

No, you can't tell him. Just forget it.

Yeah, right, forgetting was going to be a problem.

We got all the presents ready and headed over to my parents' house. I wore the diamond earrings from Luke and a cozy sweater. Bill sat in the back seat of the truck next to Molly who wagged her tail happily.

I looked over at Luke with a smile. "No riding in the truck, huh?"

His lips flashed a quick, guilty smile but he said nothing.

It had been my idea to bring Molly along to introduce her to the kids. They hadn't met her yet but after having her for a while, we realized she was good around people. We wanted her to socialize more.

I'd offered to drive in my car but Luke had insisted on his truck since it warmed up quicker than mine. Bill hadn't brought Barney which we were both thankful for considering we didn't know Molly's temperament with other dogs.

I had almost forgotten about the text I'd seen that morning as we pulled into my parents' driveway with Bill chatting in the back about the Charger. Together, Luke and I bought a new exhaust system for it as Bill's Christmas gift. I wouldn't have even known what an exhaust system was unless I had Luke.

Bill petted Molly and she happily panted next to him.

"I knew you'd get a dog eventually," Bill mentioned as Luke turned off the truck. "Dogs are about the only loyal thing we humans can find. We aren't loyal like they are."

I thought about his words and glanced at Luke. He just had a small smile on his face looking at Molly in the rearview mirror.

Loyal? Luke had always been loyal. In everything he did. But did I know him that well? Had his loyalty been an act?

No. That wasn't who Luke was.

We got out of the truck and Luke grabbed Molly's leash and she jumped out ahead of Bill. We walked to the front door with bags in hand and knocked. I felt his free hand come around my waist and he kissed my temple.

"You okay, Sweetheart?"

I nodded without looking at him.

I just had to convince myself there was no way he would hurt me.

The kids loved Molly and Molly loved them. The house was chaotic as they chased her around and around the kitchen table. My parents had bought her toys and treats, and she was happy with them all. We watched the kids open presents and Kate came over to sit next to me on the couch. She pointed to my left hand at the empty finger.

"No ring?" she asked quietly.

"Nope."

"Do you think he's asked Dad yet?" she inquired. Dad was holding Aaron as he played with a new remote-controlled car and laughing with Luke about a story.

"I don't know."

She looked at me, her eyebrows knitting together. "What's wrong?"

God, she was so much like Emma. They both knew me too well when something was bothering me.

I jerked my head to the kitchen and we both went out and refilled our wine glasses.

"I checked Luke's phone today to, you know…see his history if he's been looking at rings or anything and he hasn't, but I found a text," I said quietly.

She frowned. "There's so much to uncover in that sentence but first, a text from whom?"

"That's the thing! I don't know. It wasn't anyone saved in his phone contacts."

"What did it say?"

"'*Did she leave yet?*'"

She sighed. "Brynn, that doesn't mean it's a woman. It could be something for a Christmas gift or—"

"I know but I can't stop thinking about it, Kate! Owen cheated on me. I never once looked at his text messages or browser history or anything because I trusted him too much. What if the men I like are the same and I'm just going to repeat my last relationship?" I could hear my voice breaking and she saw it. She walked over closer to me and gently squeezed my hand.

"Luke isn't Owen. There is no comparison. He would never cheat on you because he loves you more than anything. Everyone can see that. Have a little trust," she said softly.

I felt my body relax slightly at her comforting words. "I love him a lot, Kate, I just worry about him not proposing yet. Maybe it's because he has met someone else and he's biding his time."

She scoffed. "I doubt that. Maybe it's because you've been so scared of getting remarried that he's giving you time."

That was probably it, but I didn't want to admit that.

"Just give it a few days. You'll see it's nothing," Kate reassured me. I wasn't completely convinced.

Two months passed and no one claimed Molly. I put through adoption papers with the rescue so she could officially be ours. It didn't take much convincing after three months with her. Luke was head over heels. She was his shadow most days and though she came to me for food and scratches, she and Luke were buddies.

"Just remember I saved your cold butt!" I exclaimed, handing her a treat as she took it gladly and went over to her bed.

She'd never chewed up a thing, unlike devil dog Barney, and she was sweet with everyone she met. She was the best dog we could've asked for.

Luke chuckled, signing his name as well on the adoption papers. She was ours, not his, not mine, *ours*. Part of me was a little worried about that but it was one of our first things together.

"You know what this means?" I said to him.

"Mm?"

"If we breakup we both get partial custody."

He rolled his eyes and pulled me into his embrace but made me look up at him. "There is no breakup, Clark. There will always be an *us*," he said softly.

His words melted me a little as I stared up into his gaze. I had been so busy prepping for Emma's bridal shower and bachelorette party that I hadn't focused much on Luke and the suspicious text. I'd put it aside and focused on other things because I knew it couldn't possibly be true. I hadn't been able to check his phone either lately to see if there were more text messages from…whoever it was.

What if there were more texts? What if Luke really is lying?

I automatically stiffened and stepped back.

He frowned at me as I moved over to the bag of art supplies I'd picked up to make centerpieces for the bridal shower. I'd been doing this lately. I would forget about what I'd found and pretend everything was okay then I'd remember and distance myself from him. It wasn't good and I hated myself for it, but I didn't know how else to handle it.

You could just talk to him about it.

And risk him finding out I'd been snooping on his phone? Yeah, no thanks.

"Is everything okay, Sweetheart?" He stared at me across the kitchen.

I looked up and met his gaze, forcing myself to be okay. "Yeah, everything's fine."

I could feel him staring at me, even as I plugged in the hot glue gun and pulled out the artificial flowers.

“I’m going to run some errands today since I’m off. I’ll be back a little later,” Luke informed me. He came over and kissed my head then went upstairs to change.

Molly came over and sat in front of me, her tail wagging.

“Listen, I know it’s my fault. I shouldn’t have ever looked,” I muttered to her.

She huffed and put her head down.

Luke appeared not long after going upstairs and grabbed his wallet, keys, and coat.

“I’ll be home a little later.”

“Where are you going?” I asked, looking up.

He watched me without saying anything. My heart took a leap off a cliff and not in a fun—night adventure, cop coming to rescue me—way. A cliff that fell into not water but broken, chipped rocks, and I was sure to die a horrible death.

“Sam wanted me to pick up some special bourbon for the bachelor party. It won’t take me long.”

It sounded real…it sounded legit but part of me just wasn’t sure because of that hesitation.

“Okay,” I said weakly and watched him walk out the door.

Molly whined after he left and stared out the window at him until the truck drove away.

Where is he actually going? Who is he really meeting?

I needed to get more supplies for the bachelorette party. Since the wedding was in April, we were doing it at the end of February, so I had to be prepared. It was only in a few weeks. I could run into town, too, and see about getting more hot glue sticks...and if I just happen to run into Luke....

I grabbed my purse and slipped on my shoes then bolted out of the house.

Chapter Twelve

Jumping to Conclusions and into Bushes

I was stupid. I was so, so stupid for doing this.

But I had to be sure. What if I found out today that he was? What would I do?

I caught up to Luke in his black truck but stayed far behind so that he wouldn't see me. I prayed to God that his cop instincts didn't alert him that he was being followed.

I watched him turn the corner and pull behind the restaurant called Bleu's that sat between Swan's Jewelry and the liquor store. I frowned.

Why would he park behind the building and not in front?

I quickly parked a distance away, then jumped out of the car and crossed the street. A horn honked as I hurried, but I ignored it and ran to the corner of the strip mall to hide before Luke saw me. I peeked around the corner and saw him on his phone, talking to someone and looking toward the buildings. Just then the door to Swan's Jewelry opened and out walked a woman who was also on her phone. She looked around and when she saw Luke, she smiled and waved. He returned the gesture as she put up one finger for him to wait then disappeared back inside.

Dread filled me as I stared at the door. My gaze flit to Luke who was still sitting in his truck waiting.

Waiting for a beautiful red-haired woman in the black dress.

It was confirmed...Luke was cheating on me.

"Brynn?"

I jumped and looked behind me to see Emma walking towards me, coming from one of the stores.

"Shhhh! Get over here!" I waved her over and she frowned.

"Listen, we've talked about you seeing a therapist, right?"

"Look around the corner," I whispered.

She did and her brows shot up. "Is that Luke?"

"Yes!"

"Sitting in a back lot by himself?" she asked quietly.

"Yes."

She just looked confused.

"I followed him because I think he's cheating on me."

She rolled her eyes and crossed her arms. "Brynn, he isn't Owen."

She was starting to sound like Kate. "Yeah, so obviously my taste in men hasn't changed! Do you really trust my judgment at this point? Jessica Swan just came out the back door of the store and waved at him. I think he's waiting for her now. Just come on!" I grabbed her arm and drug her over to a thicket of bushes that would give us the cover we needed. We crouched down and peeked over them. Luke was right in front of us.

"You are going nuts, Brynn! You're being absolutely ridiculous. Jessica isn't that type of girl."

I rolled my eyes. *Yeah, she was.* Emma just didn't remember her from high school.

When Luke looked up, I dropped down into the bushes for cover, dragging Emma with me. Thorns dug into my stomach and a rock was poking me in the ribs as we laid still.

"I can't believe you have me doing this with you!" she whispered angrily, trying to adjust herself to relieve her discomfort.

I turned my head to look at her and smiled sadly. "Best friends forever, right?"

She narrowed her eyes. "Someone has to love you."

"Ouch!"

"What? I'm sorry but it's the truth!"

"No, 'ouch' as in there's a freaking rock getting to second base with me right now."

We heard the truck door open and peeked up to see that Luke had gotten out of the truck and was walking towards the back door of the jewelry store.

"Brynn? Is that you?" I looked behind us and saw Kate standing on the walkway squinting at me as I lay in the bushes with Emma.

I put my finger up to my mouth and pointed. She saw Luke and I grabbed her arm and yanked her down beside me. She squealed and Luke looked over but not before Kate almost fell on top of me.

"Brynn, I'm starting to worry about your mental stability!" she grunted angrily.

"Believe me, you, and this entire freaking town! Now listen to me, Luke is right on the other side of the bush—"

"He's not looking," Emma whispered as she glanced up.

"Listen, the both of you are going to think I'm crazy but I'm not!" I whispered, looking to my left to Emma then my right to my sister-in-law.

Kate just raised a brow.

"I really think Luke is cheating on me."

"Oh Brynn," Emma said in exasperation.

"No, I'm being serious!" I exclaimed.

Kate patted my arm. "Brynn, this is your trauma speaking. Luke wouldn't do that."

"That's why I'm here, to find out," I said, looking back and forth between them. They both didn't look convinced. "A few months back Luke got a text message from a woman that said, 'Did she leave yet?'"

I was waiting for Emma to say something since Kate knew already but she was silent.

"What was her name?" Kate asked, trying to get me to tell Emma the full truth.

"Okay, so it wasn't a saved number—"

"Then how did you know it was a girl?" Emma prodded.

"Because that's a girl sentence!"

Emma and Kate just looked at me.

"Okay, there's more, hold on," I started again. "You know those earrings he bought me for Christmas? Well, it was a necklace set and I never got the necklace! Then today he just happens to need to leave suddenly, and I follow him here where Jessica seductively waves from the back door." I gestured as much as I could lying down huddled in the bushes with my best friend and sister-in-law.

"It may not be what you think, Brynn. Yes, Jess is single but that doesn't mean she's with Luke," Emma said.

I felt tears come to my eyes. "She's beautiful and definitely more stable than I am." I put my head in my hands and mumbled, "He's going to go bang her on top of the freaking engagement rings."

"Brynn," Kate sighed.

I was beginning to hate my name, especially in the tone they both were using.

We heard a door opening and all three of us quickly got up and peeked over the bushes. Luke was standing by the back door of the store as it opened and Jessica came out looking beautiful, a bright smile on her face.

They spoke quietly and Jessica's grin just grew as her eyes lit up at what he was saying.

Then he gestured his arm out towards the alleyway between the buildings to leave the back parking lot. We briefly heard them talking.

“Their steaks are great and the wine…” Jessica's sing-song voice said as they walked together closely. Before they got too far away, we all saw the teardrop necklace around her delicate neck. One that matched my earrings.

Kate and Emma glanced at each other but were quiet.

“It might not be what it seems,” Kate finally said in an unconvincing voice.

They were going out to eat together and she had my necklace. He'd parked back here so it wasn't as obvious.

I felt my throat tighten as visions of them together, just as Luke and I were together, ran through my mind. Of her being at his house as they watched TV on Saturday nights eating popcorn, and whatever came next.

“He’s not like that. There must be an explanation for this,” Emma agreed.

I fully stood up, straightened myself, and brushed the dirt and leaves from my arms and legs. My whole body felt emptied of emotion.

"I don't know what to do," I whispered, my eyes moving towards the alleyway that Jessica and Luke walked through.

"This could be another Monica situation," Emma said. "You jumped conclusions that they were together, and they weren't."

I put my hands on my hips, my eyes filling with tears. "Did that look like me jumping to conclusions?" I asked, needing reassurance but not really wanting it.

"No one in town is talking about Luke cheating and it's not like the people of Cold Spring can keep their mouths shut about anything," Emma explained.

Kate and Emma stood side by side and I realized my brother definitely had a type. They were so similar in different ways but both stared at me wearily. They gave each other a side look of concern.

I didn't register Emma's words because I was thinking of Luke. My heart was plummeting to the ground and a boulder was on top of it to sink it faster and harder.

"I have to go. Thanks for helping me," I muttered and before their pleas could stop me, I went back to my car and drove home.

Home. *Would it be home for long?* Would he kick me out as Owen did? I'd been blindsided by the divorce and the cheating but this time, I knew. What would I do?

When I got back, my adrenaline was spiking, and I went straight upstairs to our room. I clenched my hands as I looked at his neatly organized dresser and I had an urge to destroy it. Rip his clothes out, empty his cologne bottles, and take a sledgehammer to his gun safe.

I looked at his nightstand and saw not just the picture of him and his dad fishing but a picture of us. I sat down on the edge of the bed and picked up the small picture to look at it closer. The man didn't have a frame for it but a small piece of tape that was attached to the lamp. He didn't keep many pictures around the house but these two. The two people in his life he loved.

It was a day we'd gone out fishing together, but I'd made him take a picture of us outside by the Hudson with his phone. I hadn't known he'd gotten it printed, let alone on his nightstand.

Amare tu est facilis.

I'd thought it would be easy to love him. It hadn't been easy to love Owen.

I put the picture down, my hands shaking. I saw scratches on my arms and small cuts. I needed to get cleaned up. I went to the bathroom and stripped down. Then I slid under the shower of water and let out a relaxed breath. There was a knock at the door and I opened my eyes slowly.

"I'll be out in a little," I called out. My heart took a painful leap.

The door creaked open, and I saw Luke peek his head into the room. "May I join you?" he asked with a grin.

"No—"

He didn't listen and the next thing I knew he was stripped down and pushing the curtain open to come in behind me.

His smile was wolfish when he saw me, his hair mused as if he'd had his hands over it, or someone else had. I flinched at the thought and of course, glanced down below his waist.

Damn it, how was I going to stay mad at him when that *was here?*

I turned back to the stream of water as he wrapped his cold arms around me and pulled me back against him.

I swallowed.

This was too nice, too familiar. I couldn't let him erase what I'd seen today.

"I have to get out," I said hurriedly, and his arms fell as I quickly slipped out of the shower. I grabbed a towel and wrapped it around me and literally ran from the bathroom before his penis made my common sense leave my body.

I was downstairs biting my nail when Luke strolled down in sweats. He came over to me, a grin on his face as he trapped me between the counter and him, leaning his weight into me.

"Come back upstairs, we can finish what we started," he placed a kiss on my neck, his hands lifting my shirt.

I felt fluttering and I knew that was my common sense flying away or about to.

"N-No."

He pulled back and frowned at me. "No?"

"No," I said more strongly. "Where were you today?"

He stepped back and his eyes flashed something that I couldn't read.

How could I not? I should know all of his looks...why not that one?

"I had to run errands, I told you that."

"What errands?"

He paused, looking at me and I shifted on my feet. "What is this about, Brynn?" he asked, avoiding the actual question. I realized it was a tactic, one I remembered Owen using many times. Deflect the original question to ask one of their own.

I hated that he was putting me through this.

"This is about knowing where you were today. If you can't answer that, then that's a problem." I was proud of how strong I sounded.

“I told you I had to pick up bourbon for the bachelor party then I went to Tweeds where I ordered my suit for the wedding,” he explained so well that I faltered for a moment.

But I had been there…I had watched him meet Jessica.

“Oh yeah?” I demanded. “Then which clerk helped you at Tweeds?”

He frowned at me but answered. “Kyle.”

I didn’t like this. I didn’t like how this made me feel or the way I was treating him. I wanted to blurt out that I’d seen where he’d gone first but I couldn’t. I also couldn’t confirm he hadn’t gone to those other places after meeting with Jessica. He might not be lying for the most part, but he wasn't telling me everything.

“Where is this coming from, Brynn?” Luke asked, looking over my face.

Molly must have heard the tone of our voices and came over to lean against my leg. I put my hand on her head and looked down to avoid his gaze.

I couldn’t tell him I’d followed him to town and huddled in bushes with Emma and Kate, spying on him.

“I-I don’t want to talk about it anymore,” I whispered, tears coming to my eyes as Molly looked up at me with concern.

“Brynn,” Luke demanded, his voice a little sharp.

"I'm going upstairs." Before he could stop me, I ran back up to our room and shut the door.

I sat on the bed and put my head in my hands.

He had refused to tell me everything he did today and that in conjunction with the texts...*How could I trust him?* How could I believe that he wasn't lying about another woman?

I took a deep breath and steadied my breathing even as I felt like a boulder was sitting on my chest.

When I woke up the next morning, I was alone in bed with tissues scattered around me. *He hadn't come to bed. Did I really think he would after I caught him? Was this the start of our end?*

I got out of bed and went downstairs to let Molly out. I glanced over at the couch and was shocked to find Luke sleeping there under a big comforter and Molly laying between his legs. She perked up and jumped down to come over to me. He didn't wake up, though, as I watched him lying there with his eyes closed and his arm above his head. He was beautiful and my heart hurt so much just looking at him.

What was he doing to me?

After letting Molly out, I got changed to meet Emma and Mackayla at the coffee shop, Spring Awake, to talk over bachelorette party details. As I was about to leave, Luke woke up.

“What time is it?” he asked.

Not looking at him I read the time.

“Shit! I’m late for work!” He flew up the stairs behind me and I heard the shower being turned on as Molly gave me a look.

“I’m not going to feel guilty for that,” I muttered to her.

Chapter Thirteen

Drunk Girls of Cold Spring

At Spring Awake, Emma, Mackayla, and I sat in the back and chatted about the bachelorette party.

"I have it all planned out, so you don't need to worry about a thing," I reassured them. This was a much better topic to talk about than the fact that Luke had slept on the couch, and I was wondering when he'd confront me about moving out. My stomach churned at the thought and I felt my throat close.

Could I get a hold of my old landlord to see if I could rent the house again? Or would I have to start from scratch again? I didn't want to move back in with my parents.

"Brynn?" Emma jarred me from my thoughts as I looked at her and covered my fearful expression. Mackayla sipped her latte and stared longingly at Emma's muffin. She'd started dieting after she started her own wedding planning even though the girl was thin as a rail.

"Sorry, what'd you say?"

"I said we'll have to post signs tomorrow that we're closing the store on Saturday in two weeks."

"Oh, yes. We should definitely do that tomorrow. I'll print something up and get it on our social media too," I offered.

"Perfect! I'm so excited!" Emma exclaimed. She sobered a little and looked at me with a sweet smile. "Thank you for being my best friend and doing all of this. It means a lot to me."

"Of course, you deserve it, Em."

"Maybe in the near future, we'll be planning one of these for you, Brynn!" Mackayla winked and I must have made a face because she frowned. "What's wrong?"

I looked down at my coffee, so I didn't have to look into their eyes. "Nothing. I'm thinking of picking you all up at 3 p.m. and then leave right from Em's house to Albany. It's just the four of us, right?" I asked, evading the question.

I prayed Mackayla wouldn't push more because I wasn't ready to share any of that information with her. Especially the possibility of Luke and I ending things. Even when we fought before, Luke always came to bed. It was our way of forgiving each other, of not letting a fight stop us from sleeping by one another.

But it stopped him last night. *Was he distancing himself because he knew I knew?*

"Yes. Monica is staying with us, so you'll just have to get Mackayla first. Aren't you drinking?

Shouldn't we have a driver or something?" Emma asked.

"I'm not going to drink."

"Brynn! That's not fair to you," Emma whined.

"No! I love drunk Brynn! Scarlet still shares the story of Luke coming into Sullivan's, flinging you over his shoulder, and stalking out. It was so hot!" Mackayla gushed.

I rolled my eyes. That wasn't a fun hangover.

"It's okay, I promise. I'll be the mom for the evening. I've already planned it out," I said.

Mackayla pouted but Emma asked, "Are you sure?"

I knew I needed to stay sober for plenty of reasons. Albany was easy to get to, but I'd only gone a few times and hadn't ever traveled to where we were going. I'd decided not to take us to New York City for many different reasons, mainly because we were four girls alone in the city and traffic was horrible.

"It's too bad Mackayla is twenty-one already or else we could have made her our driver," Emma said, glancing over with a smirk to Mackayla.

"I don't think I want her driving us sober or drunk," I retorted which made Mackayla gasp and Emma and I laugh.

"I also have a theme," I said with a grin.

"Ooh! Is it Space Cowgirls?" Mackayla guessed.

"No, it's Roaring 20s!" I said excitedly. I had spoken with the people at a speakeasy-themed bar in Albany and based our evening off that.

"I love it!" Emma exclaimed.

Mackayla looked disappointed. "How am I going to be a sexy 1920s girl?"

"Look up flapper dresses, I think you'll be fine." I chuckled, taking a sip of my coffee.

"This is going to be fun!" Emma said with a big smile.

I hoped it would be. I'd planned everything down to a tee. I had an agenda that was going to be loosely followed but allowed us to make split minute decisions if we wanted to keep going for the evening. I only hoped it was everything Emma had dreamed.

"Will you tell Monica the plans?" I asked.

She nodded, taking a bite of her muffin. Mackayla looked at it with big eyes. "Sam used to only talk to her like four times a year, but I try to chat every week. Especially since she's in the wedding, I wanted to make sure she felt included."

"If I was a lesbian, she'd be my type," Mackayla announced.

Emma laughed and I rolled my eyes. Monica was beautiful. It was a surprise to find out she wasn't bringing a date to Emma and Sam's wedding. She'd claimed there was a guy but not one she wanted to meet the parents.

"Okay, so we need flapper dresses, what else?" Emma asked.

"Yourselves, I'll take care of the rest."

When I got home that evening, I half expected Luke to have my things packed for me, but he didn't. He wasn't even home. In the early evening when I was making dinner, he texted me to tell me he was working part of third shift for someone since he'd slept through his alarm and had missed a few hours.

I didn't text back. I ate my dinner in the living room with Molly lying on the couch with me.

I looked around the room at the pictures of us I had added to the walls and the photos of our families. So much of our life was interwoven. Even after only a year and half. We'd gone through a lot together. I just didn't understand how he could throw that away.

Normally I would have waited up for him like I had nights before. Instead, I went to bed early, taking Molly with me, and fell asleep.

Two weeks went by and Luke was quiet. We didn't say much to each other but he still kissed me goodbye and said he loved me and slept in bed beside me every night. He picked up plenty of work and there were several days I didn't see him. It was for the best I'd told myself, but I missed him so much. I missed what we'd had before.

How could we go back to that? His silence felt like a confirmation of his disloyalty. *Trust was broken…wasn't it?* I didn't know what to do. I didn't know if I should confront him again or if I should just leave. I tried not to focus on it and put my focus and energy into Emma.

The day of the bachelorette party I got changed upstairs with Molly staring at me from the bathroom doorway.

I had found a flapper dress that was black with tassels, added some fishnet stockings, heels, and a headband and I was all set. Luke called for Molly but appeared in the hallway and looked in at me.

His eyes roamed my body and I couldn't help but feel that spark of desire and butterflies coating my stomach.

"You look beautiful," he said quietly, pushing open the door the rest of the way. He leaned one hand on the frame and stared at me. He was dressed in his uniform from work, a few buttons undone and damn if it didn't look sexy.

I avoided his gaze and added more blush to my cheeks. "Thanks."

"Are you going to keep this up?" His tone was stiff.

"Keep what up?" I played dumb.

I heard him growl in his throat. "Seriously, Brynn? What is going on with you? It's been two weeks since you've given me the cold shoulder. I've given you space to work through whatever it is."

I put the blush down and stared at the sink.

How could he ask that? He knew what was going on!

Without thinking, I said, "I think I should move out."

The words left my mouth before I could stop them. I felt my heart racing as the silence continued from Luke, but I hadn't gotten the courage to look at him.

Did I want to see what was on his face? Did I really want to move out? What if I was wrong about him cheating?

I glanced over and I felt my world shifting as I finally saw his expression. It was guarded.

"Why?" His one question had my stomach in knots.

I didn't want this. I had made a mistake by mentioning it. Especially on a night like this.

"Are you cheating on me?" My question sounded broken and I hated how it made me feel.

Pathetic.

Young.

Scared.

His face contorted with so many emotions but one was surprise, then anger.

"Why would you ever think that?" he demanded.

"Because you haven't been telling me the full truth!"

"I haven't lied to you! What would I gain from cheating on you? I have fought to make you mine for years now! I'm not going to be the damn punching bag for your ex's mistakes," he snarled.

"Maybe you should be because you are just like him!" It was another regretful sentence I'd said out loud that I shouldn't have.

He flinched back from me, his brown eyes going dark and his expression flattening out. His arms fell from the frame of the door. Molly whined under his legs but he continued to stare at me. "Is that really what you think, Brynn?"

No, I wanted to shout but I felt my heart tearing in two seeing him hurt. I'd done that. I'd hurt him.

My phone went off and I jumped and grabbed for it. An excuse to stop this conversation that I didn't want to have. When I glanced down at the number, I saw it was Emma.

"Don't answer that, Brynn. We need to talk," Luke stepped into the bathroom, towards me and I paused.

His eyes were heated with anger, and I knew that if I did answer the phone, we would be over. It would end with him leaving or kicking me out. That's how it was the first time, so how was it any different now?

My heart racing and pounding in my chest, I answered Emma. "What's up? I'm about to leave."

"Do you have red lipstick? Monica and I just got ready but realized we need red lips for this event!"

Luke's jaw tweaked and one minute he was glaring at me and the next he was leaving the bathroom and slamming the door.

"Y-yes," I stuttered. "I'll be over soon."

I slipped the tube of lipstick in my purse and practically ran down the stairs, kissed Molly and left. I didn't say goodbye, I didn't say I love you. I was too upset.

I needed to forget what had happened and enjoy tonight or at least pretend to. I couldn't ruin this evening for Emma.

I got in the car and drove towards Mackayla's, pushing back tears. I tried not to mess up my makeup, but I could feel my emotions spilling over.

I was angry at myself. Was I sabotaging my relationship with Luke because I feared being hurt again? Was he really not cheating? Part of me knew there was no way he could cheat on me, that Luke wasn't like that. He wasn't Owen. But that nagging, divorced heart I still had, warned me not to believe him. It warned me to stay away from someone who might harm me, but it was already too late for that. I'd given myself completely to Luke.

My heart was already starting to shatter.

By the time I got to Mackayla's I'd pushed all thoughts of Luke away as much as I could.

Mackayla looked like a flapper with a short red dress, fishnet stockings, stilettos, and a sparkly headband. She was grinning as she got into the car and looked over at me.

"Damn, Brynn! You look hot!"

I rolled my eyes at her. "And you look like you're going to a strip club and not as an attendee."

"I know, right? Darren barely let me go." She giggled. "We may have had a quickie in the car—"

"Nothing I need to know about!" I cut her off as we drove towards Emma's.

"Oh stop, it's not like you and Luke haven't done it. I'm pretty sure your first month of being together you had hickeys all over your neck!"

I blushed. It had been really good. *Had*. We hadn't had sex in weeks now. Not since I'd caught him going to see Jessica.

I shifted in my seat. "Yeah, well I don't want to know what you're doing. You could be my little sister."

From out of her purse, she pulled a small tin container and grabbed out a mint in the shape of a penis.

"You've got to be kidding me!" I exclaimed as she offered me one with a coy smile.

"What? I knew you'd be too much of a prude to get penis shaped things, so I did the honors." She reached further into her bag and withdrew lollipops, cups, and even shot glasses with the male body part adorned on them. "See, I have more!"

"If this insults anyone, I'm telling Emma to fire you come Monday," I hissed.

She just grinned and offered the tin closer to me. "Calm down and eat a dick, Brynn."

When we got to Emma's, she and Monica had already taken a few shots. Monica was beautiful in a short gold sequin dress and heels. She decided not to wear a headband and just leave her black hair long and straight. She had on sparkly makeup that made her eyes look more gold than brown. Then there was Emma who was decked out in silver and white. She was even more stunning and twirled as the tinkling sequins of the dress made noise as Mackayla whistled.

"Looking beautiful, Emma! Almost like a virgin!" Mackayla cooed.

"Let's go before I leave her here," I murmured to Emma who just grinned.

We all got in the car, Emma in the passenger seat and the other two in the back.

"Turn on some good music!" Mackayla sang in the back.

Emma turned the radio on and found a station that was 80s female singers. It fit perfectly.

"This is going to be so much fun! Thank you for doing this for me," Emma said.

I smiled. "We'll get dinner first then we'll go to the bar. I can't wait for you to see what it is!"

"Do you want a penis mint?" I heard Mackayla ask Monica in the back.

I heard Monica laugh loudly and prayed it hadn't insulted her. Emma turned in her seat and begged for one too.

That was a good sign.

"Alright, it's 4:30p.m. it's shot time!" Monica yelled from the back.

I heard the tinkling of glasses then watched Emma out of the corner of my eye throw back her penis shot glass with alcohol in it.

"Ick! What is that, Monica?" Emma exclaimed.

"Cheap tequila," she said proudly.

"Definitely tastes like it," Mackayla coughed.

"Brynn, you'll have to have at least one shot with us, please!" Emma begged.

"Yes, when we get to the bar I will."

They all talked about the night ahead and I knew just from the conversation that Mackayla and Monica were already getting along very well. Both were young and enjoyed the art of partying.

"Mackayla, you'll be next for a bachelorette party! Do you know what your sister is planning?" Emma asked.

"You're engaged?" Monica asked with surprise beside her.

I saw a flash of Mackayla's hand in the rearview mirror and that told me she was showing off her ring. "Yes, I am! Darren asked me this past summer. I think my sister is going to do something lame, to be honest. She's not twenty-one," she pouted.

"All the guys I date are idiots," Monica said.

"I thought it was going well with you…you and…."

"Jay, and no. He's so obsessed with himself, I can't," Monica explained. "All these San Diego guys are just airheads."

"You could move back home," Emma offered.

I glanced in the mirror and saw Monica's expression change to annoyance. "I have too good of a job out there. Besides, I'm fine being single. Not everyone can find a Sam or even a Luke like you guys," she ended.

"Aww!" Emma cooed, pressing a hand to her heart.

Find a guy like Luke. This nosy ass town had not even spread a lick of rumors about him cheating. Actually…I hadn't heard anything. Guilt nagged at me as I thought too much of my conversation with Luke before I left.

I realized there was more to Monica than I thought. Maybe she was going through her own issues just like I had been…well was. I probably shouldn't have judged her so quickly.

"No more talk about guys," I instructed. "We're celebrating Emma."

The girls in the back gave a salute and took another shot.

We went to dinner and by then, all three were already buzzed. I made sure we ordered enough food, so they had plenty in their bellies before they really started getting drunk. We had a sash for Emma to wear that said "Bride to Be" and she wore it with glee.

After dinner, I drove us over to the speakeasy bar and corralled them all towards the entrance. A bouncer was standing outside the small door with a 1920s hat and pinstripe suit.

"Hello ladies, do you have the password?"

"Penis!" Mackayla shouted and she and Monica and Emma laughed hysterically. The bouncer was tall and broad and looked amused as I moved over to talk to him.

"Purple Deer," I recited.

They sent me the password after I made reservations for us. It was a busy bar, and they only allowed a certain number of people in at a time.

The bouncer nodded to me and opened the door. I walked in first and made sure everyone came in with me. The room was a small makeshift living room with a fireplace and a few chairs. There was no one there and no bar. I turned back to the bouncer as Monica went searching around the room.

"Is this an escape room? I bet I can find the door!" Monica said.

"Look at this pretty light," Emma exclaimed, touching a glass lamp that I prayed was glued down.

Mackayla went over and lounged on one of the chairs.

"What do we do now?" I asked the bouncer.

He nodded his head towards the fireplace. "There's a door, find the handle."

I went over to where Monica was and found the handle that was tucked beside the fireplace. I pulled on it and Emma gasped as music and light filled the small space.

"Go!" I encouraged as all of them went ahead into the low-lit room. Jazz music murmured through the bar and the smell of cherries and cigars wrapped around us.

There was a stone wall and an old-fashioned wooden bar with a brass handle and stools. There were small tables and chairs seated around. It wasn't full of people, but it was getting there.

"Let's get a Shirley Temple!" Emma squealed and pulled me towards the bartender.

"Yes, but we need to add some tequila to it!" Monica said as Emma ordered the drinks.

Monica turned around and leaned against the counter to look off into the crowd. "I don't do a lot of this with girlfriends, it's nice to finally have a few."

I looked at her and smiled. "I'm a little biased but I think Emma is one of the best girlfriends you could have."

Monica smiled softly and I knew it was genuine. "I didn't mean to hit on your boyfriend by the way. He was sweet and polite. Had I known he was taken, I wouldn't have even flirted with him."

I swallowed hard and looked away. I knew she was telling the truth. "It's fine. It's water under the bridge."

"I'm hoping to one day meet a guy as good as him. If you know any, send them my way," she joked.

"There's plenty of good men in Cold Spring," I encouraged. "You just have to find them."

I looked back at her and I saw hope in her brown eyes.

"Alright, are we here to talk or are we here to drink?" Mackayla demanded serving up shots from the bartender.

I think we were here to drink.

It was a fun night. I allowed myself two drinks at the beginning of the night and danced with my friends in our flapper dresses on the dance floor. A group of other ladies bought us drinks to celebrate Emma's wedding.

"I'm getting married!" Emma had shouted right before she took another shot. Then she flew into me and hugged me tightly, her skin smelling of alcohol. "Brynn, thank you for tonight, it's been awe-maze-ing!"

I hugged her back and laughed. "Wait until tomorrow to say that. I think you'll be hating me then."

"Never hate you," she said, pulling back. Her eyes were glassy and unfocused as she smiled prettily at me. "I don't even hate Kate anymore. I forgave Mark a long time ago. I'm inviting them to the wedding!"

I raised a brow. "Really?"

Emma leaned forward. "Remember when we were in the bushes together when you thought Luke was cheating on you?" She tried to whisper but it was much louder than that. I looked around to make sure no one had heard and Mackayla and Monica were out on the dance floor so they couldn't have.

"Yes."

"Well, after you left, I talked to her and it was soooo good, Brynn. She's like so nice."

My thoughts went back to Luke and my mood fell. "Well good, I'm glad you're getting along now."

Mackayla stopped dancing and waddled over to me. Her makeup was smudged from wiping her face. “I don’t feel too good, Brynn.”

“It’s time to go then,” I said.

Emma whined but I was able to get them all out and walking back to the car.

“This was the best night!” Monica sang as she crossed arms with Mackayla which was funny looking considering Mackayla was much shorter than Monica’s almost six feet.

“It was! Brynn knows how to throw a party!” Mackayla agreed.

“Ooh, look a pretty bird,” Emma cooed, walking away from me. I went and grabbed her before she could touch it.

“That’s a broken glass bottle, Em, not a bird. Come on,” I said, pulling her away.

We arrived at the car and Mackayla and Monica got in the back and Emma in the passenger seat. I started up the car and turned on my phone GPS for directions home.

“Ugh, I really don’t feel too good,” Mackayla whined from the backseat.

I got on the highway and headed down the road.

“I feel so wired like I could run a mile,” Monica said, her eyes bright and wide.

“Probably all the Trash Cans you drank,” Emma said with her eyes closed from the front seat.

"God, I want sex too. Anyone else as deprived as I am?" Monica asked.

I glanced down at my phone and saw no text from anyone, not even my siblings. I turned the screen off and swallowed hard.

"Nope! I'm getting it all the time!" Emma piped in.

"Gross, I don't want to know what my brother does," Monica muttered, running a hand through her long black hair.

Emma just giggled.

Then suddenly, I felt a weird movement from the car and I realized something felt wrong. The car bumped and bumped, and I pulled off the road and down an exit. I turned on my phone and realized I hadn't started the GPS! I didn't know where the heck we were! I could've been going the wrong way.

"What's going on?" Emma mumbled. I found a sideroad that was in the country and parked under the light then put on my four-way flashers. When I got out of the car, I saw the problem…a flat tire.

"You've got to be kidding me!" I snapped.

Emma got out and wobbled around until she saw what I was looking at. Her headband had come off and her eye makeup had been smudged. She'd also taken her shoes off and was barefoot on the back road.

"Em, get back in the car. You aren't wearing shoes!" I complained.

"What's up?" Monica hopped out of the car and looked at the tire. "I can fix it! I've got this!"

"Really?" I asked with surprise and relief.

"Yeah! Um, where's your spare?"

I opened up my trunk but glanced in to see Mackayla leaning back in the seat.

I got out the spare tire and the kit and brought it over. Monica stared at the kit and I realized…she was still very drunk! She couldn't even pick up something without reaching for it several times.

"Monica, do you actually know how to do this?" I asked.

She looked up at me and giggled until she was almost on the ground. I looked skyward then around us and realized Emma was nowhere to be found.

"Where's Emma?" I demanded, looking inside the car.

Monica stood up unsteadily beside me. "Emma!" She called into the fields and open road.

"Mackayla! Where did she go?" I asked with panic as I opened the car door. Mackayla groaned and looked at me.

"I don't know. Leave me alone!"

"Get out and help us, now!" I yelled.

I looked around the road and walked further down, my heart racing. What if we lost the bride? *Oh my God. Sam would never forgive me!* I would never be trusted again.

"Wait! Brynn, there she is!" Monica said as Mackayla came up beside us on the road.

"Emma! Stop!" I ripped off my shoes and hurtled down the incline to the field to grab Emma who was walking to the cows that were on the other side of a fence.

"I want to see the cows," Emma explained as I finally caught up to her. Her feet were muddy and she started laughing when she saw me.

"Come on, you can't be down here. This is someone's property," I explained as I steered her back towards the car.

She didn't fight me as I got her up the hill and onto the road. "This is no one's property, Brynn. It's the Earth!"

Remind me to tell her to stop watching those nature documentaries.

I got her back up to the car but Monica was trying to figure out how to get the tire off and wasn't helping. Mackayla was dry heaving while sitting on the road.

You've got to be kidding me! I felt so out of control and ready to break at any point.

"Monica! Stop!" I snapped. She jumped and frowned at me.

"I can do this. I live alone. I've lived alone. I am independent. I can do this," she repeated.

"I'm never drinking again!" Mackayla whined after another dry heave.

"Look, is that a star?" Emma slurred as she started to walk away again.

"Monica, go stop her!" I pleaded.

She did and I dropped to my knees and grabbed the lug wrench and started to unscrew the lug nuts from the tire. I'd successfully gotten three off but still had two more and by then I was sweating, I had black all over my hands and the light of the road lamp was doing nothing to help.

I growled and looked up to see Monica pulling Emma back down the road to the car, both giggling and talking about something.

Mackayla was lying flat on her back in the grass groaning.

"That's it!" I snapped, standing up. "Everyone get in the car now!"

Once I'd gotten all three women into the backseat, I locked the car and stood outside looking at the tire.

"I'm hot!" I heard Monica whining in the back seat then Mackayla burped.

I glared at the flat and the last two lug nuts I couldn't get off. It also struck me that I didn't jack up the car and I shouldn't try with all three women in it.

I growled and stood up, my eyes burning with tears. I had to call for help. I couldn't call Sam. I didn't want to worry or upset him.

I had to call Luke.

Even if I didn't know where our relationship was headed, I needed him. Would he even answer the phone? He might see me calling and be reminded that I called him Owen just a few hours ago.

I had to try.

I dialed his number and closed my eyes as I leaned against the front of the car. It was two in the morning so he may not even hear it.

He picked up on the second ring. "What's wrong?"

It's like he knew. He knew I needed him. He didn't answer upset or angry. I felt the dam burst and I sobbed out my response. "I have a flat tire, Emma keeps wandering away, Monica thinks she can fix anything but she's useless, and Mackayla—"

"No! It smells like vodka cherries!" Monica gagged from inside the car.

"Brynn! Let us out! Mackayla just puked!" Emma squealed.

"I feel so much better now," Mackayla sighed with relief.

"I'll be there as soon as I can," Luke said before I could say anything else.

Chapter Fourteen

Confessions from the Cheated

Luke showed up within the hour after I sent him our location. I knew he had definitely been speeding considering how quickly he'd gotten to us. By then I'd let the women out of the car and Mackayla had thrown up two more time while I held her hair. Emma had thrown up from smelling Mackayla's puke and Monica was green in the face, ready to vomit at any moment.

Luke pulled up to the scene and I went over to him, my tears had probably messed up my makeup and I looked straight out of a horror film. I wanted to hug Luke so tightly when I saw him, but I didn't.

His hair was ruffled like he'd run his hands through it and his jeans were slightly wrinkled. He'd probably just gotten up and threw on whatever he had. His eyes were sharp and determined when they met mine.

"Bring them to the back of the truck," he instructed quietly, and I went round them up.

Luke put down the tailgate, turned on a camping lantern, and had them hop into the truck bed. He gave them water and even brought pretzels.

"Stay here," he instructed them. Emma was almost asleep, and Mackayla was leaning on Monica who was munching on pretzels already.

"Yes sir," Monica said with a giggle, saluting him.

Luke and I walked back to my car, and I held the flashlight he gave me while he jacked it up. He was able to wrestle the two lug nuts off that I couldn't, replaced the tire, and had it all done within ten minutes. He stood back up and put the old tire in my trunk along with the flat tire kit.

"You can only drive 40 miles per hour on a spare. I'll take the car home, you take the truck with them," he said calmly, as if he hadn't just driven over an hour to come rescue me and three of my friends after a wild bachelorette party, and like we hadn't almost been on the verge of breaking up a few hours ago.

At this point, how could I even fathom that he was cheating on me? Not when he had woken up at 2am to come help me.

"I'm sorry, Luke. I'm so—"

He put his hand on my chin and made me look at him. His brown eyes were dark in the low light, but I saw the man I'd fallen in love with so easily.

"I'll see you at home."

Just those five words almost had me in tears again. It was as if the earlier fight hadn't happened, or he was saying it wasn't over.

We weren't over.

He handed me the keys to his truck, and I started walking towards the back to get the girls out from the truck bed.

"Luke," I called. He paused to look back at me. "I promise I won't let anyone puke in your truck."

His lips worked into a smirk. "I think one of them got it all out in your backseat. I'm not worried about it."

Emma, Monica, and Mackayla were snoring by the time I got them back to Emma's house. Sam had waited up and was happy to collect his future bride into his arms. He held her and she nuzzled into his neck, falling asleep.

"You guys have fun?" he asked quietly as Monica got out of the truck with a groan.

"Yeah," I muttered, not willing to say more.

He gave me a knowing smile, then walked into the house with a stumbling Monica behind him.

"Thanks, Brynn," Monica called with a wave.

When I dropped Mackayla off at her parents, she made a few grumbling noises but waved me off and went into her house.

As I pulled into our driveway, I leaned my head on the steering wheel.

I was exhausted and ready to peel off my clothes and go straight to bed, but I had to talk to Luke first.

I went into the house and Molly was the first to greet me. Then I saw Luke in the kitchen and a glass of water sitting on the counter with two pain pills for the headache he knew I had.

I dropped my shoes by the door and slipped off the stockings then walked straight over to him. He opened his arms to greet me and as soon as I was there, I felt so much emotion as I breathed him in.

What the hell was I doing? I was trying to ruin everything between us. Without even trying to hear his side of the story.

“I need to know,” I said against his shirt, not wanting to look at him. “Are you seeing someone else?”

He pulled me back and looked down into my eyes and I saw everything. Every answer to my questions, every emotion, everything that I already knew but couldn’t believe because of how messed up I was.

“No, Sweetheart. There is no one else but you.”

His words made feelings bubble up into my chest. “I’m sorry, Luke. I’m just a mess.”

No one said that being in a relationship after divorce would be this hard. No one prepared me for the number of commitment issues I'd have or the constant trust issues.

I had almost ruined my relationship with Luke not one time but wasn't I now on like a hundredth time?

"Now it's my turn to ask questions," Luke said softly, rubbing my cheek with his thumb. "What brought this on? Why would you think I was cheating on you?"

It was time to fess up.

I took a shaky breath. "Listen, I'm going to sound crazy and delusional, and you may rethink being with me."

He raised a brow at that.

"I was on your phone a few months back and I saw a text from someone, I assumed it was a woman, but the number wasn't saved in your phone."

He frowned at me. "What text?"

"It said 'did she leave yet?'"

He pulled out his phone and scrolled through his texts until he found it. He sighed and showed me. It still didn't have a person's name tied to it.

"This is from Rick at work. Mrs. Brown came in and she loves him but he avoids her at all costs. He was hiding in the breakroom until she left. He sent this out as a mass text to all the officers," Luke explained.

"But you called the number right afterward?"

"Yeah, because I wasn't at work, so I had no idea who it was. When I called, Rick explained why. I've just been too lazy to add him to my contacts."

"Oh," I said, feeling stupid but not ready to admit it. I crossed my arms ready to throw out the big thing. "I followed you one day."

This is how you get broken up with, Brynn. Not remarried in case you were wondering.

"You followed me?" he questioned, his voice rising an octave.

"You went to the back parking lot of Bleu's, and I watched you meet up with Jessica Swan. And she has the matching necklace to my earrings. What am I supposed to think? Especially since Jessica is beautiful—"

"That was you I saw, wasn't it?" Luke narrowed his gaze as I felt guilt spread throughout me.

"You never saw me."

He stepped closer, his eyes lighting with amusement. "I swore I saw you jumping behind the bushes."

My face turned red. "Back to the point, what were you doing there with her?" His lip turned up and he walked past me back into the laundry room. "Um, hello? We're having a conversation here!"

He returned a second later with a black velvet box, it wasn't a ring box though. It was a necklace box. "I was getting this made for you."

I hesitated on opening it but Luke stood with his arms crossed staring expectantly at me. I flipped it open and was stunned. It was the beautiful silver chain with a teardrop stone hanging at the end. The one that Jessica was wearing that matched my earrings he'd gotten me for Christmas.

"I didn't tell you this before but the diamonds in the earrings and this were my mother's," Luke said softly. "It took time to make the set so I've been working with Jessica since before Christmas on it. You saw me in the back parking lot because Jessica was giving me the necklace and she was meeting a friend at Bleu's so I walked her there before going into the liquor store. After I had the necklace made, Jessica liked it so much she had one like it made for herself."

I looked up with wide eyes and stared at him. "Really?"

"Remember how I said my father would buy my mom all this jewelry and she never wore it? He gave me a few of her pieces to make into something for you. Jessica couldn't salvage the original chain or earring backs so she took the stones and added them into the items I picked."

I felt like the biggest asshole. The worst girlfriend ever imaginable. I'd spent so much time doubting his commitment and love for me. Had I just opened my eyes I would've seen that he loved me unconditionally. I'd almost single-handedly ruined my relationship with him all because of Owen. Because I thought that every man had to be like him. That none could be as perfect as Luke, but I was so wrong.

"I'm sorry, Luke. I'm sorry for calling you Owen and for ever wanting to move out, it was–"

"It's okay, Brynn," Luke said softly, pulling my body into him. Like a magnet I followed, staring up at him. "I'm used to you by now."

I smacked him playfully and he just chuckled. I grew serious again as I looked up into those familiar brown eyes. "Next time I'll come to you first and talk it out."

He brushed his hand through my matted hair. "You probably won't but we'll work on that together. I love you, Brynn."

My throat felt tight as I saw the love he had for me. "I love you too and I promise I'll make all of this up to you. We have the rest of our lives, right? Because I'm going to have a lot to make up for."

He shook his head, his eyes flashing something that looked like surprise. "The rest of our lives?"

I bit my lip. "Yes, because I want to marry you, Luke. I want to spend the next sixty years together and with no one else but you."

He leaned down until his lips brushed mine. "I like the sound of that."

A few weeks went by and Luke and I felt even closer than before. The fight that almost broke us up had changed me. It was almost as if the switch finally flipped in my mind. Luke was my dream guy; he was nothing like Owen and never would be. He was my forever.

I woke up one Saturday morning to the sun streaming in the window. I reached across and felt the emptiness of the bed. Luke must have gone downstairs but Molly was there with her head resting on the edge of the bed looking at me with those large bicolored eyes. Her tail hit the floor more rapidly as I sat up and she seemed excited, like she needed to go out.

"Okay, okay, I'm getting up."

I stood and brushed my hair out with my fingers then headed down the stairs. Molly was ahead of me.

I smelled breakfast food along with coffee as we made it down to the first floor. Luke was leaning against the counter with his ankles crossed and a coffee cup in his hands. He was dressed in those black sweats with the white t-shirt, and it made my mouth water.

"Good morning," he said with a twinkle in his eyes.

I moved over to him for a lingering kiss and his hands wandered to my hips until he was pressing against me more firmly.

“Tell me you don’t have to work today,” I said softly.

“I don’t work today.”

I opened my eyes and looked at him and he saw what I wanted in that gaze. *Him.* I wanted everything from him.

“Why don’t you let Molly out first,” he suggested.

Her tail wagged harder as I kissed him again and turned to grab her leash. When I went to attach it, I saw something around her collar. It was a box.

A black velvet box that looked strangely like a small version of the necklace box that had my earrings and necklace in.

It isn’t a ring, Brynn. We’d gone through this a million and one times, right? It’s probably more earrings or maybe a ring but not *that* ring.

I pulled the box from her leash and when I turned around to Luke…he was kneeling on his left knee, his coffee cup placed on the counter behind him.

He was smiling and it set my world spinning with how handsome he was.

Molly ran over and sat beside him as he put his hand on her to stroke her head, but his gaze never left mine.

My heartbeat was erratically pounding in my chest as I realized this was exactly what I’d wished for.

"Brynn, would you—"

"Yes!" I cut him off before he could even finish the words. He chuckled and braced for me as I lunged for him, wrapping my arms around his neck, and falling to my knees.

He kissed me back with passion and love. It wasn't a grand gesture with people to show off to or in a hot air balloon, it was just us. And us was all that mattered. It was like the best kept secret, a moment in time that only we would remember.

I pulled back as we both kneeled on the ground, the box still in my hands as Luke watched me.

"That was exactly the reaction I wanted," he said softly. "Open it."

My eyes brimming with tears and my hands shaking a little, I opened the box with a pop. In the velvet cushion was a delicate silver band with a beautifully set round diamond in the center. It was stunning and feminine and simple.

It was me.

He understood me. He knew me.

It was as if it finally struck me the reality of my life with Luke. It was such a large comparison to Owen that it had me breathless for several seconds.

Luke took out the ring when I didn't move and gently brought my hand up between us. Then he put the ring at the tip of my finger but before slipping it on, he made eye contact. It seared me to my toes and my heart stopped for a moment.

"I'm glad we're on the same page now," he said with a smile as he pushed the ring the rest of the way on my finger. It felt foreign to have a ring there even though it'd only been a few years since I'd divorced. I couldn't help but think it felt *right*.

I leaned forward and kissed him and put all my emotions and feelings into just that kiss. I needed to show him how much I loved him.

Two hours later, two glasses of mimosas, one round of sex, and we were relaxing in the bedroom.

I stared at the ring. It was just breathtaking. Every time I looked at it, I saw how much Luke loved me. It wasn't just a symbol of marriage, it was of how much he knew me, how familiar and how caring he was.

Luke nuzzled my neck and wrapped his arms around me tighter. "Do you want to start calling your family?" he asked in a muffled voice.

I brushed my hand through his hair and smiled. "No. Not yet."

He lifted his gaze to look at me and his eyes were heavy lidded. "Why?" I detected worry in his tone, and it filtered through his expression.

I moved my hand from his hair to his cheek and caressed the stubble on his chin. "Because I like it being our secret. Our thing. It feels…more special and intimate. I want to enjoy this moment of blissfulness before they start demanding wedding plans, dates, and God forbid, children."

He chuckled and kissed my collarbone. "I see."

He leaned on his elbow to stare down at me and tightened his hand on my waist. "How did you not guess what I was doing after seeing me with Jessica Swan?"

I flinched and looked away. "It's my explosive nature. My tendencies to think the worst in someone, especially a guy."

"Hope the scratches from the bushes were worth almost ruining the surprise of your engagement ring," he said with a grin.

I opened my mouth in surprise and looked at him. "Wait, what?"

He winked at me. "I wasn't just having her design your earrings and necklace. Your engagement ring was what I was actually picking up that day."

My heart tightened at his confession. The day I thought he was cheating on me was the day he was doing the opposite.

"I'm so sorry, Luke. I'm just–I'm so messed up. Who even does that? Or even looks through their boyfriend's phone?"

He chuckled and kissed the crook of my neck.

"Fiancée. And if you ever want to look at my phone, I give you full permission. I have nothing to hide, and I want you to feel comfortable."

I felt my nose burning and my eyes sting. He shouldn't have to do all those things, but he does.

"You are a good man, Luke Price."

I held his cheek and kissed him.

Chapter Fifteen

Wedding Bells and Wedding Hells

Later in the day we called my parents and told them the good news and they were ecstatic, especially my dad, which wasn't shocking.

"My baby girl is getting married!" Mom cried through the phone.

"Again," Dad said offhandedly which made me roll my eyes but laugh.

Mom knew me well enough not to ask a ton of questions but let me live in the moment.

When we hung up with them, I decided to three-way Lauren and Kate to tell them. They squealed with joy and asked tons of questions about how Luke did it and, of course, wedding plans that I hadn't even begun to think about.

"So, everything is…okay between you two then?" Kate asked and Luke gave me a raised brow.

"Yes, all a misunderstanding," I responded.

Kate murmured "I told you so," while Lauren completely missed it. "You know what this means?" Kate added.

"What?"

"He's going into the sibling group chat!" Kate announced.

"Oh no," I muttered, and Luke looked over at me. "Be prepared," I mouthed to him.

After the call with Kate and Lauren, it only took a few seconds for Luke to get a text.

Kate: Welcome to the Clark sibling group chat!

Dylan: About time you propose. We thought we'd have to force you guys.

Lauren: It's so exciting! Glad to have you here! I was the most recent one added and let me tell you, it's a blast!

Mark: Brynn, don't screw this up. We like Luke.

Me: Shut up, Mark.

Dylan: We're taking Luke if ya'll break up. We love you sis but….

Luke: Thanks for the welcome.

Luke glanced up as I filled our wine glasses. "How do I mute this shit? I keep getting text messages every second," he muttered, annoyed.

I chuckled and went back over to sit beside him on the couch. I showed him where to mute and he let out a relieved sigh.

Emma was next to call and Luke leaned his head back on the couch as it rang.

She answered, sounding tired. She'd been working on all the wedding planning on top of working full time at Feather Blue.

"Hey Brynn, I'm at the store. What's up?"

"I'm sorry about your car, Brynn!" I heard Mackayla yell out in the background.

I hadn't heard or seen much of her since the bachelorette party, and I thought it was perhaps because she didn't want to clean her puke out of my car.

"Tell her she still needs to clean my backseat," I said sharply.

Emna laughed. "I'll tell her when I've cornered her."

"I actually have news." I looked at Luke who sipped his wine with his arm thrown over the back of the ouch. "Luke proposed."

Emma was quiet for a moment. "What did you say?"

"Yes, of course!"

"Oh, thank God!" Emma exclaimed. "I was hoping you weren't going to be that dumb! I'm so happy for you, Brynn!"

Luke heard her comment and chuckled quietly.

"Send me a picture of the ring! Also, what decorations can I set aside for you? Do you know where you want to have it? Or when? This is so exciting! I promise to hold your hair while you puke after your bachelorette party, too."

I just laughed. "I don't have an answer to any of that. Get back to me within a week and I may."

"I'm so happy for you Brynn," Emma said softly. "See, getting remarried isn't all that bad!"

I looked at Luke whose lips were quirked into a smile and that made my stomach warm. "No, it isn't."

Lauren and Dylan had a baby girl, Evelyn Marie, and we all visited her a week later. She and Dylan were ecstatic and to my surprise, already great parents.

Luke and I were on cloud nine for the entire few weeks. Our relationship was better than ever.

I went to meet him for lunch at the station and was greeted by a few of the officers and the secretary.

"Brynn! Congratulations!" the older woman said.

I thanked her and then Shane Brown came out to grin at me. "Heard about the engagement. Congrats, Clark. We all wondered when it was going to happen. Luke had been going to Swan's so many times we thought he was going to buy the entire store!"

I snorted. *And I thought he was boning the owner.* "Well, he did a good job picking it out."

"Do you need a florist? My cousin down the road makes some beautiful boutiques," the secretary asked.

Where the hell was Luke? I looked around the office but didn't see him or Sam.

"Oh, um, I don't know yet."

"Oh yeah, Rick is a DJ on the side; I'm sure he'd give you a good price," Brown offered.

I could feel myself getting overwhelmed with all the questions. I started to remember my first wedding and almost broke out in hives. My ex-mother-in-law had her hand in everything I did. The week of my wedding, I barely slept, trying to make sure everything was perfect just to please her and it was perfect. Nothing crazy had come up and the day had worked out smoothly. Looking back, I realized it was a wedding event. It wasn't two people who loved each other coming together. It was a giant ceremony to show off.

"Um, thanks. I'll keep it in mind."

The secretary was just about to add something else, but Luke saved me by walking around the corner. I couldn't help but feel my heart do a quick *thump-thump* at how he looked. Powerful and strong in his uniform and when his gaze met mine, his grin made my heart thump a little harder.

"Hey, you're early."

He leaned down to press a kiss to my lips and lingered for a moment before drawing back.

"Where do you want to go?" I asked.

I reached for his hand, and we waved to the others in the office and left. "The diner?"

We were stopped three more times by people from the town congratulating us and offering their assistance for our future wedding.

We hadn't even gotten to the diner, and I was already overwhelmed again.

Luke's hand was on my back as we rounded the corner and I saw the restaurant was full of townsfolk for lunch.

I stopped in my tracks. "I think I'm not hungry anymore."

Luke chuckled. "Why?"

"I'd love for everyone to stop trying to plan our wedding!"

He turned towards me and made me look at him. "They are just being nice because they support us. You don't have to take their suggestions because, in the end, they are just suggestions."

The first time, I had to take my ex-mother-in-law's advice or else she wouldn't have paid for anything. This time, the only people paying for or organizing our wedding were us.

"Okay, you're right."

We went into the diner and were seated quickly. Several people came over to chat with Luke, but he tried to nicely dismiss them to spend more time with me.

"Not trying to add fuel to the fire but have you thought about what you want to do for a wedding?" Luke asked as he reached across to take my hand.

I sighed. "I've thought about our wedding a lot. Even if I didn't want to, the whole flipping town has forced me to." Luke just shook his head with a smile. "Do you even want a wedding?"

He shrugged. "I want what you want."

I raised a brow. "That's not an answer, Luke. Well, okay, it's an answer but it's not a helpful answer."

He chuckled and took a sip of his coffee. "You'd spare me if it we just had a small wedding or even eloped."

That was more of the answer I wanted. "I can work with that. But I don't want to do anything until Emma and Sam are married."

"I'll agree if—"

"If what?"

"If you either let me wear the same suit for their wedding as we do for our wedding or if we make it casual."

I tried to pretend I was contemplating it to make him sweat but then broke into a smile. "Deal."

He grinned and squeezed my hand lightly.

It was the day before Sam and Emma's wedding and Luke and I were relaxing on the couch watching TV, drinking our coffee.

I propped my feet over his legs and he ran a hand up my thigh and winked at me. I smiled and shifted a little.

He took a sip of his coffee and turned to watch the weather. "It's going to be nice this weekend."

"Perfect for a wedding," I said, taking a sip of my own.

Molly sighed and leaned her head against my foot that rested on Luke's knee. "He's mine."

Luke just shook his head, not even glancing at either of us.

I couldn't believe that this was where I was in my life. I'd thought that my happiness was gone, and I wouldn't find someone good. I had been so wrong.

Feeling a little sentimental, I leaned over and kissed Luke's cheek. He turned and smiled as I ran a fingertip over his jaw and the stubble that grew on his chin.

"What?" He asked.

"I love you, Luke."

He raised a brow, but I saw surprise and happiness shine in his eyes. "What do you want?"

I bit my lip. "That's a loaded question."

He put down his cup and took mine and my stomach swirled with anticipation. As soon as both cups were safely out of reach, he turned and grabbed me. He pushed me onto the couch and fell over top of me as I laughed. He took that opportunity to kiss down my neck and across my chest. His hands held my hips as he went lower and lower.

My phone buzzed in my back pocket but we both ignored it as he started to peel away my shirt. It stopped when my breath left me as his kisses were now on my bare skin and I ran my hands through his hair.

I sighed and closed my eyes, arching into his familiar touch.

The phone buzzed again in my back and Luke growled and looked up at me. "Who is calling?"

I groaned and grabbed it from behind me and saw Emma's picture.

"It's Em."

He moved back with a glare towards the phone and even I was angry at her for ruining our moment.

"Hey, what's up?" I answered, trying not to sound as if I'd been about to do the deed.

"I'm freaking out, Brynn!" Emma's voice was high pitched, and I immediately went on high alert.

"What's wrong?"

"My contact is stuck in my eye! I can't get it out and Sam is picking up his tux and Monica...well Monica is nowhere to be found!" She breathed in a shaky breath and I heard the sobs. "Please Brynn, please come help!"

"I'll be right over."

Luke didn't hesitate to encourage me to go, and I did quickly, grabbing my dress for the evening, just in case, and driving quickly to Emma.

She had a washcloth pressed to her right eye when she opened the door but her left eye was red and tears streamed down her cheek.

"Brynn!" she cried out as she reached for me. "I don't know what to do or where to start! I'm such a mess!"

"Shh, it's okay. Let's get your eye taken care of first. Who is your eye doctor?"

Once we got an emergency appointment with her eye doctor, I got her into the car and drove towards town.

"Now, where is Monica?" I asked as Emma leaned back in the seat.

"She went out last night with a few old high school friends and never came back home. Sam and I have called her multiple times, but she isn't answering!"

"Did Sam let the station know?"

"You can't file a missing person until 48 hours after they were last seen."

I gritted my teeth. "This stupid town is too nosy for someone to go missing anyhow." I thought of an idea as I pulled into the doctor's office. "Can you get in the building by yourself?"

She sniffled. "Yes. Are you waiting out here?"

"No, there's something I need to check on. I'll be back to get you soon."

Emma's right eye got watery again. "Thanks for being my best friend, Brynn."

I smiled. "I'll be right back."

I burst through the doors of Sullivan's and the normal afternoon crowd was there along with Scarlet.

She raised a brow as I rushed over to where she stood behind the bar, polishing glasses.

"Can I help you?"

Scarlet and I weren't on the best of terms. Ever since I'd gotten so drunk that one night and she'd called Luke on me. But I wasn't here to be mad at her.

"Was Monica Locklear here last night?" I asked.

She watched me for a moment. "What if she was?"

I wanted to roll my eyes at her. "She's missing. Sam and Emma are freaking out because she didn't come home last night, and their wedding is—" I looked at my phone. "26 hours away. It's important, Scarlet."

She sighed. "Fine, fine. She was here until I closed at 2 a.m. She was with Sophie, Vince, and Alex. From the sounds of it, she was headed home with Alex."

"Alex Elichberger?" I confirmed.

She nodded.

"Where does he live?"

"Do you really think—"

"Scarlet, you know everyone's business. You can't tell me you don't know where he lives!" I snapped.

She narrowed her gaze. "He lives at 4554 Broad Street."

I smirked and slipped her a twenty. "Thanks."

I bolted out of the bar and headed toward Broad Street. I glanced at the time and knew Emma would probably be ready soon so I had to make this quick.

I knocked loudly on the door, hoping to God she was there.

"What?" I heard a man yell out before the door whipped open. A young guy with black straggly hair answered with a towel wrapped around his waist and nothing else.

"Oh for the love of God!" I snapped, covering my eyes. "Is Monica Locklear here?"

"Yes, get her out of my house, please. She's been sleeping on my couch all night," he growled and when I uncovered my eyes, he was stalking back into the house. I looked in and saw her sleeping curled into a ball on the black couch.

I went into the bachelor pad and leaned down to look at Monica. Her makeup was smeared, and her black hair was a mess. Somehow though she still looked like a runway model.

"Monica?" I whispered, touching her hand.

"Mm, five more minutes," she mumbled, squeezing her eyes shut.

"Monica, it's Brynn. You need to wake up."

Her eyes blinked open and she sat up straight almost scaring me. "Oh my God, what time is it? Did I miss the school bus?"

Too annoyed to laugh, I watched her look around the room, trying to find something familiar. "No, Monica. You're like twenty-five. You were partying last night. I need you to come with me so we can get you cleaned up for the rehearsal dinner. It's in—" I looked at the time again. "Three hours."

"Oh shit," she groaned, smacking a hand to her forehead. "That's today."

"Come on, let's go."

I pulled her to her feet, and she still towered over me as I helped her get her shoes and go out front to the car. I got her in the back seat where she laid down.

"Blah, I hate drinking."

I snorted as I drove back to get Emma. She was waiting outside with.... "Is she wearing an eyepatch?" Monica asked from the backseat.

"Tell her she looks pretty, and sit up please," I grumbled.

She did as I asked when Emma opened the door and slid in. "They got it out, but the doctor wants me to wear this for—Monica! You found her!"

Emma looked ecstatic as she glanced into the back seat to see her.

"Yeah, yeah, I'm here," Monica said, holding a hand to her head.

"Where were you? We've been trying to get a hold of you!" Emma chided.

Monica pulled her phone from her small purse and must have realized it was off because she threw it onto the seat. "I don't know. I went back to What's-His- Face's house and fell asleep on his couch."

"What's-His-Face?" Emma questioned.

"Alex Elichberger," I added.

"Yeah, him." She made a waving motion as she wiped makeup from under her eyes.

"Did you sleep with him?" Emma asked.

"Gross, no. He's just a jerk," Monica all but growled.

Emma turned back to me and smiled. "Thank you, Brynn. Truly. I owe you my firstborn."

I pulled out of the parking lot of the eye doctor's and headed towards Emma's house. "Godparent sounds better."

"You look beautiful, stunning, runway ready," Monica said belatedly as she leaned her head back onto the seat, shutting her eyes. She missed my annoyed glare in the rearview mirror.

When we got back to the house, Emma happily went to start getting ready, not even bothered by the eye patch.

I followed behind Monica to the spare bedroom where I helped her get the dress out for that night and even grabbed a pair of shoes. She groaned and laid down on the bed.

"Nope, not today. You need to get up and get in the shower," I said strongly.

She groaned again but sat up, opening her tired eyes. "Why are you helping me?"

I looked at her and saw her vulnerability. She was a sweet person, but I could tell she was going through her own issues.

"Because you're Emma's sister so you're family."

Her eyes looked slightly glassy for a moment before she blinked, and it disappeared. "I'll go get a shower."

"Monica!" We both flinched from the deep voice as Sam yelled back the hallway.

"Well, that's my sign that I have to go tell him I failed again at life. I'll be right back." Reluctantly she moved into the hallway and met Sam.

I grabbed my bag and pulled out my earrings and necklace from Luke.

"Where were you? Em and I were trying to get ahold of you for hours," Sam whispered in an angry tone.

"I'm sorry. I got caught up and my phone died." Her voice was monotoned as if she wasn't fully in the conversation.

"You're twenty-five, Mon, you need to—"

"Grow up? Stop failing? Stop disappointing Mom and Dad?"

"That's not what I was—"

"Don't pretend it's not what you were thinking. Listen, I have to get ready for your wedding rehearsal, so excuse me," Monica said, and I cleared my throat as she walked back into the room.

She was frowning and I could see she was upset but she didn't say anything as she walked into the bathroom and shut the door.

When we got to the church for the rehearsal, Luke was waiting at the door and when he saw me, his eyes lit up. I wore a simple floral pink dress and pink heels to match along with the diamond earrings and necklace that were his mother's. He noticed them right away.

"You look beautiful," he said as he touched the necklace and reached down to kiss me.

"Get a room," Monica muttered as she strode past us in an unseemly mood, but I didn't take offense even when Luke raised a brow at her.

"She's had a tough day. Give her a break."

Emma waved as she walked toward us, wearing her beautiful white dress and heels, sporting an eyepatch, Luke looked even more surprised.

"Do I want to know how today went?"

My mind played over the events of the day with Emma's eye doctor, demanding Scarlet to tell me where Monica was and the craziness of wrangling everyone home, I decided to keep it sweet and short.

"Nope, and I think elopement sounds like a great idea for a wedding."

Luke laughed as he threw his arm around my shoulder, and we walked into the rehearsal.

The day of the wedding was in full swing. Emma's eyepatch was gone, and Monica's mood had lifted, especially when Mackayla showed up with champagne and orange juice. They quickly made their drinks then sat and got their hair and makeup done. I paused in front of a beautifully made-up Emma and smiled at her.

"Just some advice, slow down and enjoy it," I said quietly.

Her eyes grew glassy as she nodded. "Thank you, Brynn. It means the world to me that you've been so much help. I promise I'll do the same."

"I'm not doing this to get something back, Em," I said with a laugh. "And honestly, I think we're going to elope."

"Aww, really?" Mackayla complained from across the room. "No bachelorette party?"

I snorted and the hairdresser gave me a disgusted look at the noise. “Yeah, no.”

Mackayla pouted and Monica was too involved with her drink to say anything.

The morning went quickly and before we knew it, we were all swept away to the ceremony and lined up at the back of the venue.

Emma fiddled with her veil and her beautiful lace dress.

I handed out the fresh bouquets, giving Emma hers last. Her bouquet was of beautiful purple flowers with a touch of greenery and smelled amazing. The florist had done a wonderful job with them.

“Are you okay?” I whispered.

I never had time before my wedding day to really think about how I felt. I remember being nervous but not about the actual getting married part. I was worried about everything going smoothly because if one little thing wasn’t right, my ex-mother-in-law would never let me forget it. I remembered her glaring across the room at me wearing a flashy, teal-colored way-to-short-for-her-age dress, that looked like a high school homecoming dress.

“Yes, I’m fine. It’s just hitting me,” Emma explained. I saw her emotion and understood. “I’m marrying my best friend. I get to spend the rest of my life with him.”

I smiled and rubbed her arm. “Yes. You do.”

I hadn't felt that way the first time. I didn't have the time to think about who I was marrying, just about the stupid wedding, the food, the flowers...I didn't get to step back and really see why I was getting married. Of course, at that point, maybe I would have realized he wasn't right for me.

"Alright ladies, we're ready!" A lady wearing a headset said as she braced open the doors.

The music started and Mackayla went first, then Monica. I stepped in line after giving Emma a quick hug and walked into the room. As I moved forward, my eyes went to one person, and his eyes were looking right at me. Like magnets, they locked and for a moment, I almost stumbled.

Luke looked stunning with his hair neatly trimmed, wearing a black tux and the shiny shoes I'd picked out for him. His brown eyes looked over me with a very heated gaze as it roamed over my lavender dress and heeled legs. When his gaze met mine again, I felt like we were the only people in the room. It felt so intimate, and I almost walked right to him but remembered where we were at the last moment and quickly moved to stand beside Monica. His gaze didn't waver, even after I stood across from him and saw Sam expectantly waiting for Emma.

Luke smiled softly at me, and I smiled back. We finally broke eye contact as everyone was asked to stand for the approaching bride.

I glanced into the audience and saw Kate and Mark sitting and watching as Emma walked in slowly with tinkling music in the background. She was stunning in her long flowy lace dress and cathedral veil. I heard Sam's intake of breath and looked over to see his eyes looking glassy as he watched his soon-to-be-wife.

My heart ached a little at that and then I saw Luke again and he only had eyes for me.

Soon...soon that would be us and I knew without a doubt he would look at me that same way.

I quickly turned my gaze back to Emma but from the corner of my eye, I noticed someone sneaking in the side door.

The tall blonde-haired man's eyes met mine and my jaw opened in shock.

No...you've got to be kidding me! This has to be a nightmare!

There, standing at the back of the room, was Owen Rally.

Chapter Sixteen

A Blast from the Past

"You've got to be shitting me," I muttered under my breath in astonishment.

Someone cleared his throat, and I realized the pastor had heard me. My cheeks grew warm.

I looked back out to the crowd and saw Owen standing off in the corner looking at me.

Why was he here? How did he find me?

He looked as he always did in jeans and a polo shirt with his hair perfectly styled. Just like the country club boy I'd always known. It honestly sickened me to see him. That's when I realized how much I'd changed. He used to be attractive to me, now he wasn't. He was just a rich, preppy boy who'd drank too much at college and lived a privileged life. And he was definitely someone who I really, really had no desire to see ever again. My last memory of him was his shocked expression as my fist collided with his nose in the courthouse.

I flexed my hand as if it still hurt.

It didn't make sense why he'd show up here today of all days. Unless...his stupid mother had sent him because she couldn't get through to me.

I was so done with the Rally family. I'd be damned if they ruined this day for Emma and Sam.

I turned back toward to the bride and groom and watched as they recited their vows.

Owen disappeared sometime before the ceremony ended and Emma and Sam left in their getaway car for pictures at a park down the road. Kate stopped me and Mark was frowning, looking around the area, as I walked toward the car to go meet Emma and Sam for pictures.

"Brynn, did we see Owen or was that my imagination?" she whispered.

I put my hand to my forehead and rubbed. "Yes. And no, it wasn't your imagination. I have no idea why the hell he's here but he better be gone for good."

"It was him?" Mark demanded.

"I'm sure there are thousands of preppy blondes in polos in this world, but I know Owen and that was definitely him."

"Brynn!" Luke called across the parking lot waving at me to meet him.

"Does he know?" Kate whispered.

"No, not yet. Listen, I have to go. I'll see you at the reception."

I ran towards Luke and he stretched out his hand and I took it happily as we got into the car and drove over to the park.

We posed for pictures in various positions and with different people of the bridal party. It was a lot and my face felt as if my cheeks would hurt by the end of the day from smiling so much.

Luke stood beside me for several photos of just us with Emma and Sam and his hand tightened around my waist.

"You're tense, everything okay?" he asked close to my ear.

I swallowed but kept smiling as the photographer's flash blinded me for a second. I didn't want to bring up Owen, not right here with Emma and Sam. Hopefully, he wouldn't show himself again and would just leave, seeing that I was happy and had moved on.

"Sick of smiling and I'm exhausted."

His chuckle was low, and I felt it more than heard it.

"You can't be too tired," he said, his lips ghosting over the shell of my ear. "I have plans to slip that dress off you tonight."

Goosebumps formed over my neck and arms, and I leaned back into him. "I'm looking forward to it."

We got done and went to the reception hall and were seated next to Emma and Sam at the large table. Food had been served and drinks had been passed around. There was laughter that rang out and music blared. When someone tapped on their glasses, the happy couple would lean in for a long kiss before gazing into each other's eyes.

Luke's arm slid around my shoulders, and I moved a little closer to him.

"That's going to be us," I said softly, drinking my wine.

"Yes, it is," he agreed. "Speaking of, did you decide on a day yet?"

I glanced at him. "How opposed are you to September?"

He arched his brow. "Like next September?"

"No. This September?"

He looked even more surprised and turned his body towards me just a little more. "Is that what you want?"

I took his free hand and felt the familiar calluses as I looked into his brown eyes. "I've never been sure of anything, Luke, except you."

He slowly nodded. "Elopement?"

"Absolutely. I'm not going through this shit again," I pointed behind me at Emma who'd brought along her eye patch to put on after the reception.

Luke just laughed. "You tell me when and where, and I'll be there."

I kissed him then and if it wasn't for the people around us, I would have leaned in for a deeper one.

It was true. I was only ever sure of one thing, and it was Luke. He was everything I'd hoped to find in a man. Even though I almost messed things up thinking he'd cheated on me, he didn't waver. He knew me better than I knew myself.

The music grew louder and the wedding guests, drinks in hand, started to dance and sing. It was then I looked towards the back and saw *him* once again.

Owen was searching the crowd for me.

No. Not again.

He cannot be here, and I won't allow it. I tensed all over, but Luke was on his third beer and didn't seem to notice. I had to get Owen out of my life once and for all and if a punch in the nose didn't do it, maybe a second was due.

"There's something I have to tell you, Luke," I said, trying to speak above the music.

He glanced down, his arm tucked around me.

"Owen is here, and I don't know why but I have to go handle him."

He looked confused but I didn't hesitate to explain. I would tell him after I got Owen out of my best friend's wedding.

I threw my napkin on the table and walked towards the exit. Owen's eyes still searched until they landed on mine.

He grinned, a stupid, familiar one that used to make me melt but now just made my hands tighten into fists.

"Brynn, I wanted to talk—"

I shoved him out the doors quickly until he was standing outside in the warm spring night.

"What the hell is wrong with you?" I demanded. "My friend just got married and you show up twice!"

His blue eyes flared. "I thought it was you getting married! That's why I came."

I narrowed my eyes, my hands still clenched. "It's none of your business even if I was getting married. You need to leave, *now*."

"No," he said, stepping closer. I put up a hand to stop him. "I want you back."

I scoffed. "Your mommy already came and pleaded for you and it didn't work then, and it won't work now. I was done with you two years ago, Owen. There is no going back."

Owen took a step closer again, his expression hard to read as he stretched out his hand to brush back my hair. I grabbed his wrist and shoved it away.

He then saw the diamond on my hand and glared. "You're—"

"Engaged? Yes I am. So, there's not a snowball's chance in hell I'd ever want to be even thirty miles from you. Leave, now!"

Suddenly the doors burst open, and a commotion started as Luke came barging after Owen with Sam hot on his heels, grabbing for his shirt.

Owen backed away from me, looking scared.

"Get the hell out of here!" Luke raged at him.

Sam finally caught his arm and held on. I'd never seen him look that angry.

Owen straightened his spine and glared at Luke. "Who are you?"

Luke didn't like Owen's tone but Sam kept a good grip. "I'm Brynn's fiancé!"

"Well, I'm her husband!"

"*Ex*-husband!" I interjected quickly. "I've moved on, Owen—"

The doors sprung open again and Mark came out looking like he was about to throw a fist.

Owen's eyes widened more as he saw the oldest Clark brother.

"You! Get the hell out of here!" Mark snapped.

Luke didn't even turn, he kept his eyes focused on Owen.

"You get five seconds," Luke threatened.

"I can handle this!" I yelled at Luke and Mark with annoyance.

Behind me, I heard footsteps and saw Dylan rushing toward us with the same glare Mark had.

"You son of a bitch!" Dylan yelled, pointing a finger toward Owen.

"For the love of God! Stop! I am dealing with this!" I snapped at them before they could say anything else. Then I narrowed my eyes at Mark. "You had to text Dylan? Are you serious?"

Mark didn't even pay attention to me, so I sighed and looked at Owen. He was glancing nervously at all the men behind me.

"We're done, Owen. I told your mom that last year. I've moved on and am happy, so you need to understand that. You cannot come back here again."

"If you do, I'm going to do worse than punch you in a courthouse office," Luke's threat was bold, and it was more of a growl. Owen tried not to look at him, but he did and I saw fear reflect in his eyes.

"We'll help him," Dylan muttered deadly.

"I need closure, Brynn," Owen said softly, looking at me sadly.

I knew that face, I recognized it. I'd only seen it a few times when Owen was at his worst. Once when his grandfather died and again when he'd realized he'd failed the LSAT. For a moment I hesitated, but then I grew hard again.

"Your closure is that I'm done, Owen. Whatever things you need to work out, work them out with your therapist. I'm not part of it."

He glanced at Luke, my brothers, and even a helpless Sam before curling his hands into fists and walking away.

Sam let out a relieved breath and dropped his grip on Luke. "Shit, I thought he'd never leave."

"I'm so sorry, Sam." I put a shaky hand on my head and turned towards the group of angry men. "Emma doesn't know, does she?"

Sam's shirt was unbuttoned at the top since the reception had slowed and his eyes were a little hazy from the beers he'd drank.

"No, she doesn't know."

"Good, go back in and enjoy your wedding," I encouraged, seeing Luke was still riled up. He wouldn't even glance in my direction. Then I looked at my brothers. "Go back home Dylan, and Mark, go in and get Sam a drink."

Dylan muttered something and Mark gave a tight nod as they dispersed.

"Whatever you think you were going to do to him, it would've gotten you kicked from the station. You can't afford to do that, think about it, man," Sam said softly to Luke.

Luke didn't say a word as Sam disappeared back into the building with Mark.

"I don't know—"

"His mom came to see you?" Luke demanded as soon as my brothers and Sam left.

"Yes, right after you got shot. She came to my house but it wasn't a big deal. I sent her Louis Vuitton ass out the door."

"You didn't think it was a good idea to tell me?"

It struck me then...Luke was mad at me...*me*!

"N-no, it wasn't a big dea—"

"Wasn't a big deal?" he demanded again. "I can't believe you, Brynn."

I'd never heard him speak to me this way and it caught me so off guard. He actually looked hurt and upset.

"She was my ex-mother-in-law, who's the worst person imaginable! What am I supposed to say to you?"

"That she showed up and there was a possibility of your ex coming around too!" he snapped, running a hand through his hair. "I thought you were better than that."

I stared at him, unable to say anything for a moment. He was really hurt. "Luke, I didn't keep it from you because I'm hiding anything—"

"It sure looks it," Luke cut in. "I can't be around here." He strode off through the parking lot and I watched his rigid back the whole way, feeling my chest tighten with worry.

I didn't know what to say, or what to do. He'd never been this upset before.

When I walked back into the wedding, I felt in shock. Luke had just taken off. Without me.

Tears filled my eyes as I collected my purse and shoes. Emma was just a little tipsy as she skipped over to put her arm around me.

"My best friend! Are you leaving me already?"

I sniffed. "Yes, I'm sorry, Luke isn't feeling well and I need to go check on him."

She pouted. "Poor Luke. Go to him, he needs his future wife!"

I kissed her on the cheek and waved at Sam who quickly came over to get his wife.

"I'm going after Luke," I whispered.

"He took off?"

I nodded, tears filling again as I took a breath in. "He's really upset."

"It'll be fine, Brynn. He just needs time to think everything over."

I hoped he was right. I hoped that he was just drunk and overreacting and that the hurtful look in his eyes wasn't from me. Because I loved him so much and I had never wanted to cause him that much hurt.

"Oh, and watch her, she tends to wander off when she's drunk," I mumbled before leaving.

Chapter Seventeen

Cake Makes the Heart Hurt Less

I left the wedding and when I looked at my phone for the first time all day, I saw the text messages in our group chat.

Mark: *Shithead just showed up.*
Dylan: *No way…seriously?*
Kate: *Yep.*
Lauren: *Shithead, aka Owen?*
Dylan: *There isn't another shithead. It's the one and only. You need me to come by?*
Mark: *Looks like he showed up again here at the reception. I'm about to confront him. Dylan, get your ass down here now.*

I growled and swiped the messages away, not wanting to see what else had been said. I immediately called Luke's number but he didn't answer. When I got home, his truck wasn't in the driveway, and I felt my stomach sink.

I went inside and let Molly out and filled up both her and Felix's bowl. I fiddled with my ring, moving it back and forth as my throat felt tight.

I should have told him. Even if it was in passing, I should have told him she visited me.

I had no idea that Owen would show up though. It'd been several years since our divorce, why would he show up now? I thought of his hurt filled expression and how lost he'd seemed. No longer did I have any sort of feelings except that I pitied Owen Rally.

I let Molly in from outside then sat on the couch in my dress and watched out the front windows. Felix came and cuddled up next to my legs and Molly put her head on my knee.

Would he come back? He had looked so hurt and thinking about it again gave me a pang of regret and sadness. I never wanted to hurt him.

Lights flared over the windows, and I sat up, almost throwing Felix off me. I ran to the front door and threw it open as Luke got out of his truck and I saw his tie was undone and his shirt was unbuttoned. He stopped at the foot of the steps to look at me.

His expression was hooded as if he'd placed a wall around himself.

"Luke, let me explain, please," I begged.

He didn't say anything as he broke eye contact and walked past me into the house. He went straight to the cupboard, got out the whiskey bottle, and poured himself a shot as I shut the front door.

"She came to visit me to see if I'd take him back. I told her hell no because I was in love with you."

His back was still toward me as he took a sip of his whiskey. "When was this?"

I was ready to tell him every last secret I had. No matter how relevant it was to us. I would never keep anything from him again in my life. "It was a few weeks after you were shot. It's another reason I didn't want to mention it. You were recovering, I didn't want to add more to it."

"How long ago did he show up?"

"Today, at the wedding was the first time I've seen him since the courthouse. I've had no contact with him since then. I've only seen his mother and just that one time."

Luke's back seemed to relax a little and I stepped closer behind him.

"I didn't tell you to withhold information. I didn't think it was important. I realize now that it was stupid to not tell you."

He rubbed a hand over his mouth and turned around to face me. I saw vulnerability and fear in his eyes.

"You aren't the only one with ex issues," Luke said quietly.

I stepped closer until I could reach my hand out to graze his arm, encouraging him to continue and also because I needed to touch him.

He looked down at his feet as he spoke. “My ex-girlfriend, the one I proposed to, broke up with me a little after she said no. A year later, she tried to come back into my life, but I found out she and her ex-boyfriend were still talking. It created a rift between us, and I lost all my trust in her. I knew it could never work after that.”

I put my hands on his cheeks and tilted his head to look at me. I saw fear and need in his deep brown eyes.

“Lucky for you I had a shitty ex-husband and want nothing to do with him. I promise you that I did not encourage him to come here and try what he did tonight. I have no plans of meeting with him or giving him closure or whatever he wanted.” I slid my hands down his neck until I had them on his chest. “I want you, Luke. I don’t want anyone else but you.”

He looked into my eyes and saw my genuineness. He kissed me then, a quick one but I kept him there, slowly, tantalizing him as his hands dropped to the satin of my hips.

I pushed off his jacket and let it hit the floor with a flop. He picked me up and sat me on the counter in my bridesmaid dress and kissed me harder.

I gasped as his lips trailed down my neck, his hands reaching behind to unzip the dress as he went.

I paused and pushed him back to look into his eyes. "I never want to hurt you like I did tonight, Luke. I can't handle that again. Seeing you upset like that…I promise I will try to never do that again."

He let out a shaky breath and leaned his head against my chest, his hands wrapped around my thighs.

"Only you could hurt me that much." He pulled back and looked at me with vulnerability in his gaze. "You hold my heart in your hands, Brynn. You always have."

My body warmed at his declaration, and I traced my fingers over his chin. "*Amare tu est facilis.*"

He leaned in and whispered across my lips. "Loving you is easy."

A week later I opened the store with Mackayla while Emma was still on the last few days of her honeymoon.

When Makayla walked in the door, I knew something was wrong right away. Her eyes were puffy and red, and she wasn't her vibrant self. She had tissues in her hands, and she wouldn't look at me as she came to the back of the store to put her lunch away.

"Mackayla," I said softly and followed her. "What's wrong?"

She leaned against my desk and I saw something familiar…hurt and pain.

"I…Darren called off the engagement."

My jaw fell open at the news. Mackayla and Darren were young and in love, but feelings can change quickly at that age. Emma and I both knew that but always tried to be supportive and encouraging.

"Oh, Mackayla, I'm so sorry." I reached for her, and she quickly wrapped her arms around me and sobbed.

"I-I just thought we'd last forever, Brynn," she cried. I rubbed her back comfortingly.

"What happened?"

She pulled away and wiped her eyes. She had no makeup on and looked like a young girl and in reality, she was.

She sniffed. "He just came over last night and told me he wasn't ready to get married then left. I tried texting him and calling but nothing." Her eyes grew wide and she looked at me. "Do you think there's someone else?"

I had a sneaking suspicion, but I didn't want to say that if I was wrong. It could also very well be that his parents talked him out of marriage.

"I don't know. But why don't you go home and take the day off?"

She shook her head. "No, I can't go home, Brynn. My room has pictures of us all over and everything reminds me of him. I need to get my mind on something else."

I sighed, knowing she was doing the right thing. The last thing I wanted to do was stay in the house Owen and I had shared. It was probably good that the asshole kicked me out.

"Okay. Why don't you unwrap the new shipment we just got in? I know you love doing that," I said, rubbing her arm comfortingly.

Her eyes lit up. "It's like Christmas."

By the time our part-time employee Niki came in, Mackayla seemed a lot better but at the end of the shift, she hesitated.

I collected my purse and saw her wavering by the door, glancing at me. "Um, Brynn?"

"Yeah?"

She wrung her fingers together, her eyes brimming again with tears. "Could I come hang out with you some more? I promise I won't stay late. It's just…you've been through this, and you give such good advice. I really don't want to go home right now."

I softened and couldn't deny that her words had made me feel good. I put my arm over her shoulders.

"Yes, we'll order in pizza."

She looked grateful and swiped the tissue over her nose again. "You're such a good friend, Brynn."

I called Luke as we headed to the house with Mackayla behind me in her pink car.

"Hey, are you off work?" Luke answered. "I was thinking we could take Molly to the park by the river."

"So," I started. "Mackayla is coming back with me. Long story short but Darren broke off their engagement last night and she's a wreck. She asked if she could come over and I said yes."

He was silent for a second. "What do I need to do? Vacate the premises?"

"As long as your name isn't Darren, I think you're safe. Could you order us a pizza, please?"

"Of course."

He was the perfect man.

"Luke?"

"Yes?"

I pressed my lips together. Was this wise to even ask? "You're not—"

"Absolutely not. You're marrying me one way or another, Clark."

I laughed in relief. "We'll be there shortly."

We pulled in and went into the house to find Luke filling two wine glasses. He smiled sadly at a bare faced Mackayla, and she looked guilty when she saw him.

"Oh, Luke, I'm so sorry. I didn't mean to intrude on your evening," Mackayla's voice squeaked.

"I got these ready for you two. This one is yours," he encouraged handing a glass to Mackayla, then one to me.

She looked shocked then tears streamed again. "You're so nice," she sobbed. "I need to find me a Luke."

Molly, not knowing what to do, stood by Mackayla staring up and wagging her tail. "You're so pretty," Mackayla said, petting her head.

I mouthed a "thank you" to Luke who seemed a little uncomfortable with the whole crying female thing.

"Go sit, we'll get the pizza." I pushed her gently towards the sofa and Molly jumped up beside her as she sat down. Molly was good at comforting people. She was the best girl.

"I decided that picking up sounds better than ordering in. I'll be back later," Luke mumbled as he leaned in to kiss me. I quietly laughed but grabbed his shirt to hold him for a second longer to look into his eyes.

"I love you, Luke."

He kissed my head, winked, and left the house.

Luke took longer to get the pizza than normal, and I half wondered if it was just to stall so he didn't have to come back to a blubbering young, brokenhearted girl.

We sat on the couch with a fluffy blanket and Molly between us as Mackayla sniffled a few times. She had wanted to watch a movie about hating men so I'd turned on a famous one that I knew she'd like. She loved it and even laughed a few times.

I heard the front door squeak open, and Molly jumped off the couch to greet Luke. Not only did he have pizza but a few grocery bags.

"I'll be back," I whispered but Mackayla didn't hear me, she was too focused on the movie. I met Luke in the kitchen, and he placed everything on the island.

"I'm assuming you were just trying to get out of coming home so soon?" I questioned with a smirk.

He raised a challenging brow, then showed me what was inside the bags.

Ice cream, a small cake, and cookies.

My mouth dropped as he shrugged. "I didn't know what she would like but girls like junk food after a breakup, right?"

My heart swelled with pride and love. *How could I ever think he didn't love me? How could I think he'd cheat on me?* Because a woman could easily see how beautiful he was inside and out and try to take him.

The protective side of me roared for a second, but I settled it down and walked right into his arms to hug him.

"You are the best man I could have ever found."

He put his arms around me. "It's just junk food, Brynn," he said, sounding a little worried.

I shook my head on his chest. "It's more than that."

"Is that cake?" We let each other go as Mackayla stepped into the kitchen and had her eyes only on the cake.

"It's yours, go ahead. Forks are in the drawer," Luke encouraged.

She went to grab a plate, but Luke waved a hand. "You don't need a plate, live a little."

She smiled big for the first time that evening as she grabbed a fork and the cake. "You're right. It's not like I need to fit in a wedding dress anymore. I can eat whatever I want."

She happily took her small cake back to the couch where she crossed her legs and resumed the movie. This time, she laughed out loud in a few places as she slowly ate her treat.

"Thank you," I quietly voiced.

He rubbed a hand down my back and smiled. "Let me get you a bowl of Rocky Road. I can at least supervise you while you're eating it."

Chapter Eighteen

I Had to Marry the Nice Guy

Mackayla fell asleep on the couch and I didn't have the heart to wake her up. I called her mom and let her know where she was and who she was with. Her mom loved me for that and said so a few times.

"I'll have her drive home first thing tomorrow."

When I hung up, Molly and I headed upstairs where Luke was watching a TV show eating a handful of peanuts. He patted the bed and she launched herself up and settled down by his feet.

"If I wake up with a peanut in my back, I'm going to yell at you," I muttered as I changed and slipped in under the covers next to him.

He chuckled and put the nuts away before pulling me against him. The TV flickered with light all around us.

We'd never had a TV in our room when I was married the first time. It was my rule. I didn't want it to infringe on our sex life. Because of that, he'd just stayed in the living room until late watching whatever he wanted while I slept alone.

It was strange how much had changed and how things adjusted, depending on the person.

A TV in our room hadn't affected our sex life in the least and he would gladly turn it off if I asked. I didn't want too though. He enjoyed it.

I'd been young and dumb and made decisions that didn't help my marriage. This second time around, I was a completely different person, and I was marrying a different man. We had learned from past mistakes, and we had a second chance to make this one better than ever. I liked my odds with Luke.

Would it have been the same if we'd met years before? Probably. I just wouldn't have known what I did now.

"I can hear you thinking, Sweetheart."

I smiled against his chest. "How can you tell?"

"You're quiet."

I smacked his side and he laughed. "What are you thinking about?"

I sighed. "If we had dated back before we met our exes, like Mackayla's age, would we have lasted? Would we have a strong relationship like we do now?" I glanced up and saw him thinking.

"I've changed a lot since I was in my twenties. I was stupid back then and had no patience." He looked at me and an amused smile crested his lips. "I think you were my true test of patience. How long was I willing to wait for a woman who I was in love with to be in love with me?" Before I could say anything he added, "I thought maybe I just had a knack for falling for girls who didn't want me, like I was some pathetic guy who couldn't find someone who wanted him."

My heart stung a little at that and guilt threatened to swarm me. I put my hand on his cheek and rubbed my thumb along his stubble.

"I've wanted you Luke, always. My heart did, my body did, it was my mind I was fighting with. I reacted badly when I thought you were cheating on me. If I hadn't acted like that, it would have meant I didn't care about you. I never did that with Owen. I let him go, but you…I wasn't willing to do that. It's also why I didn't confront you about it. I was scared of losing you, and because I didn't want to believe it."

He leaned closer and kissed me softly. It wasn't urgent or desire driven, it was just filled with love and tenderness.

"I'm just glad we aren't in the dating world anymore," I whispered.

He chuckled and the rumble vibrated my hand on his chest. "Yeah, me too. I hated it. I'm glad we're past that stage," he said with a sigh. "I'm sure Mackayla will be fine. She's young and pretty. She'll find someone else soon enough."

I sighed. "I know that, but I think she just needs to hear it a few more times."

Oh crap, I thought. How was I going to tell Emma? I didn't want her coming back from her honeymoon all excited to plan Mackayla's wedding, only to find it wasn't happening. That would open the wound that Mackayla was trying to mend.

I'll call her before work and give her a heads up, I decided. She can tell me all about her honeymoon and get it out of her system before coming in so Mackayla won't have to hear as much about it.

"The Bahamas?" Luke's statement pulled me out of my thoughts.

"What?" I turned my head to look at him, but his eyes were closed.

"The Bahamas have elopement packages. I looked up a few things today."

"Isn't that a bit expensive?" I asked, surprised that he was looking.

He shrugged, his eyes still shut. "Not really. They do discounts if you stay longer for your honeymoon."

A honeymoon in the Bahamas? I could do that.

Emma and Sam had gone to Mexico for ten days and she'd sent me pictures of amazing blue ocean and the beautiful bungalow they were barely leaving.

"Who do we want there?" I asked, as he placed his hand over mine.

"Parents, siblings, best friends, and Molly."

I laughed. "Molly can't come to the Bahamas, Luke."

He growled but it was sleepy sounding. "She's family."

"Family that you said couldn't get on the couch, bed, or truck." I glanced expectantly down at a sleeping Molly then up at Luke.

"Yeah, yeah," he mumbled. "She's different."

"We aren't taking her to the Bahamas, Lucas."

He didn't say anything else, and I felt his breathing even out.

I sleepily closed my eyes.

Where would we get married? I only had four months to plan if we were doing it in September. Hurricane season too, I thought belatedly. Maybe we'd get a discount?

First thing tomorrow, I'd research it.

A few days passed and I didn't research anything for the wedding. The store was busy and with Emma's return, everyone wanted to know about her honeymoon and of course the bigger question—when will we see Locklear babies? Emma, glowing from her honeymoon, answered with smiles and “we don’t knows” to everyone and didn’t seem too tire of it. I, however, was getting very tired of it.

“Shirley, she just got married two weeks ago, let her enjoy married life!” I finally snapped.

Shirley sniffed and glared at me. “I’m looking forward to your wedding, Brynn Clark. Then you’ll be asked the very same questions.” She turned her back and left the store with her bags of clothes.

“Brynn, it’s okay. I don’t mind the questions,” Emma explained as she printed reports for the store.

“Yeah, well, I’m sick of it. I’m going to get coffee. Do you want something?”

“Ooh yes! A frozen mocha please!”

I left Feather Blue, headed to Spring Awake and got in line to order. Mrs. Brown somehow got behind me and she tapped my shoulder expectantly.

“Good to see you, Brynn! We heard Emma is back from her honeymoon. I’m assuming you’ll be next! I’m so looking forward to being at your wedding. Lots of us from Cold Spring didn’t get to come to your first so it’ll be nice to attend the second one,” she ranted.

I raised my brow. *Did Cold Spring think they were getting invited to our wedding?*

“Um, we’re doing a destination wedding,” I said.

Mrs. Brown's mouth dropped open. "Oh, I thought you'd do it locally! You wouldn't expect all of us to spend tons of money to go to your wedding far away. That just wouldn't be right!"

I laughed but it was dry and without humor. "We don't expect everyone to come. It's going to be small and who knows, maybe in the Bahamas? But either way, we've decided to make it just friends and immediate family."

Mrs. Brown looked offended and she was about to add something when I excused myself quickly and moved up to order our drinks.

I didn't want to be rude but I hated that people thought they would be invited or they thought we should do a wedding their way. I wasn't doing that this time around.

Before I even got back to Feather Blue, my phone was buzzing with texts.

Lauren: *I just heard from someone that you and Luke are eloping to the*

Bahamas? Is this real?

Kate: *I just heard the same thing from the babysitter.*

Dylan: *The Bahamas huh?*

Luke: *What? Who said this?*

I growled and put both cups into my one arm so I could text.

Me: *Mrs. Brown thought we should have this big wedding and we were expected to invite Cold Spring. I told her no and may have said we were eloping to the Bahamas.*

Nosy, stupid people! No wonder I moved out as soon as I could. God, my mood was awful today.

Lauren: *We just had a baby Brynn…we don't have that kind of money to go.*

Mark: *What if you get married at Mom and Dad's instead? It'd be cheaper and all of us could attend.*

Kate: *I have some ideas, I'll call you later Brynn.*

No, no, *no*! This was finally the wedding I could plan. Not anyone else.

I didn't respond. I walked back into Feather Blue and gave Emma her coffee which she gladly took.

"What's up? You look upset?"

I shoved my phone back into my pocket. "Nothing. Just wedding things and people."

"You guys know what you're doing yet?"

"No, but apparently the town does. Mrs. Brown expects us to have a big wedding and invite all of Cold Spring. Luke and I want to elope to the Bahamas or someplace else," I muttered, taking a sip of my coffee. It was then I saw there was a note on the cup that said, 'can't wait to see you in white!' from the barista.

"Wow, the Bahamas?" Emma said with surprise.

"I don't know. Luke looked it up but it was just an idea. Now the town thinks that's what we are doing and my sisters can't afford it. It's a mess." I rubbed between my eyes.

"All that happened just since you left?" she asked, surprised.

I nodded.

"What do *you* want to do, Brynn?" Emma leaned on the counter and looked expectantly at me.

I pressed my lips together. "I just want to marry Luke. I want to be his wife and I don't want something big like my first one. Honestly, if my family wouldn't get mad at me, I'd ask him to forget a wedding and just go to the courthouse."

"Luke doesn't want that?"

"No. He'd want his dad there and my family," I groaned and rubbed my face. "Why couldn't I have a small family or even be an estranged family member?"

Emma laughed. "You're being ridiculous, Brynn. Your family loves you and obviously wants to be a part of your special day. And honestly…after our expensive wedding and honeymoon, we couldn't go to the Bahamas either."

I just put my head down onto the desk and Emma rubbed my arm.

A customer walked into the store, the bell ringing at the top, so I straightened and came behind the counter next to Emma.

She smiled and greeted the customer, but the lady glared at me as she shopped.

"Yikes, you've pissed off some people," Emma mumbled.

"I have no idea why, either!" I snapped, not caring if the lady heard me.

"Well," Emma started, carefully. "Luke is kind of the town hero. He saved Sam, he's been great with the community, and he's very likable.

I groveled. "I *had* to find a nice guy."

Emma tried to cover her laugh but failed.

"I have a proposition for you," I stated as soon as I walked in the door. Luke was preparing burgers for the grill and glanced up with a raised brow.

"Oh?"

I dropped my purse, slipped off my shoes, and gave a head pat to Molly before stepping into the kitchen. "Let's go to Niagara Falls and get married. Just the two of us then we come home and plan a big reception and invite everyone and by everyone, I mean *everyone*."

He took the dish towel off his shoulder and braced two hands on the counter to look at me. "You really want to do that, without your family?"

"After those text messages today and this stupid town, I just think we're better off just the two of us." I didn't mean for my voice to break, but it did.

Luke tilted his head to the side. "Mrs. Brown got to you?"

I cleared my throat. "Doesn't matter. I want to do this, just us."

"You sure?"

"Yes. I don't want anyone to know though, okay? And I mean *no one*. Not my parents or Bill or Emma or Sam. We'll plan a fake wedding on September 24th, but we'll go get married on September 17th. Deal?"

He looked at me for several seconds and I saw him fighting saying yes. He was hesitant and I wasn't sure why.

"If you're positive this is what you want, I'll say deal."

"I'm positive."

He put out his hand and I shook it as his lips curved up at the edges. "I still want you to buy a dress."

"I think I can manage that," I agreed with a smile.

Chapter Nineteen

Finally Mine

A month went by and we told my family of our 'wedding' planned for September 24th at our house. We decided to rent tables and chairs for the backyard, and we were also getting a local caterer. It seemed too easy to plan and easy to tell my family about it.

I went looking for a wedding dress alone one day but not in Cold Spring. I'd ventured out to Albany instead so prying eyes weren't around. At my first wedding dress appointment, the whole entire Rally clan had been there, dictating what I should or shouldn't wear. This time, it was just me and that's how I wanted it.

There was a pang of guilt when I thought of Emma not being with me for it and how she'd most likely be the only one upset. My mother had *been there, done that* for three weddings, four if she counted her own.

I walked into the small boutique and was greeted by a young woman in a black dress. She smiled at me.

"Hello, can I help you?"

I explained I was getting married in September and a few details about our elopement. She looked a little nervous by the timeline, but I knew I could find a dress without many alterations.

She sent me out to look alone and I found myself wandering around looking at expensive dresses. Some were breathtaking and too flashy. My first dress had been decked out in sparkles and lace. When we'd gotten our photos back, I'd taken one look at myself and realized it didn't look like me. The hair, makeup, dress, and accessories had not been me at all. I'd allowed myself to change for one day and I never got many photos printed because of it.

Not this wedding day. This time, I would print every photo, I would show off who I was and the man I was marrying because he was the right one.

I paused as I looked at the clearance rack and saw a short lace sleeve. I pulled it out gently and saw the plain satin white dress with a V-neck and a cap sleeve. It was fitted down the body and had a slit on the side. I turned to look at the back and saw a zipper concealed behind fake, covered buttons and a lace back. Overall, it was stunning. It was everything I wanted. Mostly plain, fitted, and easy to get on by myself.

"Did you find a few to try on, Ms. Clark?" the young woman asked.

I pulled out the dress. "I found one."

It fit perfectly. Like a glove. I didn't need any alterations, not even to the length since I was planning to wear heels. The only lace was on the sleeves and the low back which was gorgeous and breathtaking. It was simple and I liked that. I knew Luke would too.

I happily took it home and hung it far in the closet in the spare room and told Luke not to go in there. He was surprised I'd found one as quickly as I did.

"I'm thinking we can set up the backyard with some lights too for the evening," Luke mentioned that evening.

"I like that idea. I found a photographer today, so she'll come with us to the Falls and be here for the reception," I added.

He smiled at me and reached across the table to hold my hand. "You sure you want to do this without family?"

I'd thought a lot of my family throughout the day as I made plans and it had felt weird without them. "I think so. It will be easier for everyone if we don't make them go through the whole wedding thing again."

"But is it what you want, Sweetheart?"

I looked down at my food. I had felt like a burden for everyone when it came to getting remarried. They had a lot going on in their life and here I was about to make them go through more.

They don't tell you that getting remarried is sometimes more stressful than the first time.

I looked back up. "I think so."

Another month went by and I quickly got everything planned for both the ceremony and reception. It was nice that it was two separate events and on different weekends, it almost made it easier.

Emma and Sam were busy getting settled into married life, so I'd only been able to see her when we worked. Even my family was busy. Lauren and Dylan with my new niece who was the apple of their eye. Kate had been busy with the kids during the summer and Mark had planned a few weekend trips. My parents still checked in with us and we still had family dinner at their house, but we never brought up about the wedding ceremony.

Bill was planning to come stay with us the weekend of our reception, so I'd gotten the room ready.

Luke had been put in charge of finding us a hotel in Niagara Falls and I'd gotten our bags together for the weekend. I'd put through our marriage license and found a pastor. All of it was coming together.

The closer we got, the more guilty I felt and the more sad I was. I knew it was too late to invite my family and friends so I decided to stick it out and let it go.

After being on the phone in the living room, Luke got off and came over to me in the kitchen. "Molly can come with us," he stated with a grin.

"How?" I said shocked.

"The hotel allows dogs, and we have a wedding room booked that overlooks the falls."

I shook my head in surprise as he smiled. "You impress me more and more every day."

September 17th finally arrived, and after making sure Felix was set for a few days with plenty of food, water, and the television on to keep him company, we got our things packed into the truck and with Molly between us, we left Cold Spring.

Luke held my hand and rubbed his thumb across my knuckles.

We were doing it. We were getting married. We didn't have a rehearsal dinner or bachelor parties or any nonsense. It was just us.

It still felt weird without Bill or my big family, but again, I pushed those feelings away.

"I booked us separate rooms for tonight," Luke mentioned, and I turned to face him.

"Why?"

He shrugged and I saw a flush come to his cheeks. “I want to see you for the first time when you’re walking down the aisle. I know we’re not doing anything else traditional, but I’d like to keep that part.”

I smiled slowly. “I think I can do that, however, on our wedding night we also get separate bedrooms.” Luke looked so offended I started laughing. “I’m kidding!”

He shook his head with a grin. “Listen, we aren’t ‘officially’ married unless we consummate it and I have every intention of doing that.” His hand grabbed my thigh possessively and a twirl of excitement floated through my stomach.

We were quiet for a few moments as we got onto the highway and headed west.

“How are you doing with your family not being there?” Luke asked softly. Molly sighed and rested her head on our joined hands.

I didn’t want to admit to him that I was feeling a lot of regret about it. My family loved us and I knew they’d probably be hurt that we were doing this. It hurt me a bit too. I had to remind myself that this was just about us. Our wedding was about us becoming one and sharing this moment together just the two of us, was okay.

I looked over at him. “Luke, when our parents are gone, and our family and friends have made their own lives, it’s going to be us. It will always be us after this weekend,” I said softly.

He didn't say anything but nodded and squeezed my hand just a little tighter.

Five and a half hours later we arrived in Niagara Falls and checked into our hotel. The staff loved Molly so much they had placed a cot in the one bedroom and added a bone, bowls, and a toy.

After we settled into rooms that were connected by a door, we went to visit the room we were getting married in.

Hand in hand, we strolled into the large room with giant glass windows that overlooked the beautiful falls. There was an arch with flowers on it and a few chairs with little decorations but who needed them when the view was its own decoration? The ceilings were high and when we both said "whoa," it echoed beautifully.

A young woman who looked to be twenty-five in a uniform for the hotel came in behind us. She grinned as she saw us staring blankly at the room.

"It's breathtaking, I know. We have already spoken to your photographer, and she's seen the room. The pastor will be here about an hour before the ceremony, and we have someone setting up music for when you walk down the aisle. Is there anything else we can do to make your wedding day any better?" she asked.

"I don't think so, it's even more than what we expected," I said almost in a whisper.

Luke and I looked at one another and I could see happiness radiating through him. It reflected my own.

"Good! That's what we like to hear."

That evening after we went to dinner together and went back to our own rooms, I hung up my wedding dress and laid out my heels, jewelry, and got my makeup ready. I was doing it all, including my hair.

There was a soft knock at the suite door in the room and I went over quickly to open. Molly raced in under my legs and stood beside me waiting for a pet, Luke didn't come through the threshold but stood just on the other side.

"It's not safe for the groom's eyes in here," I said with a grin.

He raised a brow. "I wanted to say goodnight. I'm going to try to go to sleep before long." He paused and looked over at me. "You're doing okay?"

I frowned slightly but kept my smile. "What do you mean?"

He chewed on his cheek for a second and I saw his expression grow vulnerable. "No cold feet?"

I realized why he was nervous and scared...he thought that I would bolt. That I'd change my mind and leave him at the altar. With my track record, I couldn't even blame him, but it made me love him all the more.

I stepped closer until I had a hand on his chest and his arm wound around me.

"Nope. They are nice and toasty actually and I'll make sure to wear socks the whole night." I winked playfully at him as his lips turned up into a smile.

"You want Molly to stay with you?"

I sighed and patted her head as her tail hit the floor harder. "She's your buddy. Let her sleep with you tonight."

We kissed and I shut the door between us reluctantly. I laid down in bed and shut off the lights. I heard the TV in the other room turn on and a sitcom murmured through the thin walls. I closed my eyes and reached over and came up empty on the other side of the bed. I hadn't realized how much I'd relied on sleeping beside Luke so much. Hearing him snore, even if it did keep me up some nights, had felt like home. *He* felt like home.

I turned on the TV, too, hoping maybe that would help me sleep but as I lay there and tried to bring sleep in, it didn't come.

I looked at my phone and bit my lip. I couldn't believe how quickly I'd become so attached to Luke and his warm body next to mine as I slept.

I tossed and turned for over an hour until finally I rolled onto my back and sighed heavily. I grabbed my phone and called Luke. He answered on the second ring not sounding the least bit tired.

"You okay?"

"You did this to me."

There was a pause. "What would that be?"

"I can't sleep without you next to me. Whose idea was it to sleep separately tonight?"

He chuckled. "Come over."

I didn't hesitate. I got out of bed and went into the next room. Luke was sitting up in bed with his shirt off and Molly was curled at the end of the bed. I quickly slid in next to him and he lifted his arm.

"It was a good idea in thought," he said, kissing my forehead.

"I'll leave right away in the morning," I murmured as I felt sleep suddenly pulling on me now that I was with him.

The familiar murmur of the TV and his breathing lulled me. I rubbed my hand across his chest and slid it lower with a coy smile.

He chuckled and stopped me. "I'll have you know I'm saving that until I'm married."

I snorted unladylike. "Sure you are."

He tilted my chin up so he could kiss my lips. It was slow and sweet and made a tingle run over my body.

A cold nose touched my hand and Luke winced as it hit his stomach. When we gasped and looked, we saw Molly staring at us with wide eyes.

"Alright Mother Teresa, we won't," Luke muttered.

I giggled and laid my head against his chest to sleep.

No one said that getting remarried would be…this easy. I'd found my person and after a while of finding my commitment, knowing I was supposed to be with him, just felt right. He was everything I didn't have and everything I hadn't known I'd needed until after my divorce.

All those thoughts had been rolling through my mind as I finished up my makeup and hair. The photographer took lots of pictures and had me pose in different ways.

When she was finished with me, she headed over to Luke and Molly. I stood in front of the full-length mirror and stared at myself in the long white dress with short sleeves. I looked like a bride.

I'd done my normal makeup but with a bit extra of longer lashes and a darker lip color. I'd left my hair down and curled with a veil that was a little below my elbows.

I looked like myself.

I didn't look like a wanna-be magazine bride or a model that someone else had decked out. I was me.

I looked like Brynn…. Brynn Price.

Just that thought made tears fill my eyes.

I was marrying Luke. I was finally marrying a man who should always have been the first one, the one who I was always meant to be with.

We'd been through a lot in just the few years we'd been together. Luke dealing with my post-divorce issues, him getting shot, me fearing he was cheating on me and my ex trying to come back into my life. But in the end, we'd fought through it all and came out stronger than ever. He was who I wanted to be with my entire life. He was my forever best friend and the most important person in my life.

Friends would come and go.

Family would spread out to have families of their own.

But Luke...he was my life and my world, and I was privileged to be his wife.

I wiped the happy tears away, trying not to ruin my makeup as the young woman, Sabrina, the hotel wedding coordinator, knocked on my door. She had an earpiece in and when she saw me, she grinned.

"You look beautiful! We're ready for you."

I followed her out of the room, my heart racing as excitement grew in me.

"He's waiting for you. The music has started, and your photographer is ready."

It hit me then that I was walking down the aisle alone. My father wasn't there to be beside me like he'd done the first time. My mother wouldn't be there watching with tears shining in her eyes. Mark and Dylan wouldn't be there to try to act manly but still be emotional about their only sister getting married, or my sisters-in-law watching with pride. Even Emma, my best friend who'd become like my sister over the last few years wouldn't be there.

"Are you okay?" the young woman asked as we got closer to the entrance of the wedding hall.

"Yes, just wishing my family was here. That's all."

She smiled at me. "Your husband is a good man."

It struck me that she called him my husband and that shocked me for just a second until we turned the corner and I saw a man waiting by the closed doors.

I thought for a moment I'd conjured him up by thinking of him but when my father saw me and smiled, I knew he was real.

"Dad? What are you doing here?" I asked, running over to hug him.

"We're opening in two minutes, Brynn!" Sabrina announced.

Dad was dressed in jeans with a nice button-down shirt and looked casual, but my shock was still evident.

"We wouldn't miss this," he said, looking me over with a smile as his eyes looked teary.

"We?"

The doors opened as I clutched my father's arm and in the seats on either side was all my family. My mother, my brothers and sisters-in-law, my niece and nephew, Emma and Sam, and Bill. They all stood as we walked in, and I felt my eyes shining bright with tears as I realized what Luke had done. He'd brought our families here. He knew I would later regret not having them here and fortunately, he hadn't listened to me.

When my eyes finally focused on Luke standing under the wedding arch, I saw his emotions when seeing...me? No one else had ever looked at me like that.

Luke...he saw me, wanted me even for all my flaws, which were many. He loved me unconditionally no matter how crazy I'd gone. And now, with inviting my family to our wedding...it was almost too much to take.

He was it for me. He was my forever and if I didn't realize that before, it was so cemented into me now.

We got to the front and our pastor, an elderly man who I wasn't even sure could see us, asked my father who was giving me away.

"Her mother and I," my father answered. My mother dabbed her eyes as she watched, wearing a beautiful light pink dress.

The pastor nodded and I took Luke's hand, and my dad went to sit down with my mom.

They both smiled at us.

I looked at Luke and he was incredible. He'd shaven and slicked back his hair. The white button-down shirt looked like it'd been tailored to him along with the black pants and shiny shoes. He was my everything.

"Thank you," I whispered to him.

He squeezed my hand. "They all wanted to be here. I couldn't say no."

I glanced at the room of our family and felt my heart ache with happiness. Emma was under Sam's arm, and she was glowing beautifully as she wiped away tears. Molly sat in front of Dylan who looked teary-eyed as Lauren held my niece. Kate, Mark, and the kids were smiling at me. Aaron was trying to reach across to pet Molly. My parents and Bill looked at us with love.

This was the perfect day.

I turned back to my future husband and knew looking into those brown eyes that he would always be everything I wanted in life.

"Loving you is easy," I whispered.

Getting remarried wasn't bad after all, especially if it was to the right one.

Epilogue

I stood on the balcony of our hotel in the Bahamas and breathed in the beautiful sea air. The sun was warm, and my skin felt tight from a nice sunburn after swimming in the blue water with Luke the day before. We'd come back, ripped off our suits and had taken our time in the big shower together.

Our reception back in Cold Spring had been perfect just like our wedding day. The towns folk had all been invited and all brought a dish to share. We'd set up lights in the backyard, hired a DJ, and danced until 1am. I had to admit, the people of Cold Spring weren't as bad as I thought. They'd supported Luke through his gunshot injury and even more as I took care of him. Even though I didn't want to do a big wedding, I was glad we had the reception and celebrated with friends, family, and Cold Spring.

I felt strong arms wrap around me tightly and Luke's head rested on my shoulder as he kissed the bare skin on my collar.

"What are you doing out here? I thought we were napping?" His voice was more like a growl that left my insides mush.

I laughed. "Is that what they call it now? Napping? Mm, that's new."

He nipped my skin and I jumped and yelped. He kissed it and soothed me as I settled in his arms. "I was just looking at our view thinking of home."

He sighed. "It seems this week went by a little too quickly for me," he murmured.

I rubbed his arm. "I know but I miss Molly. I wonder how Sam and Emma are doing with her."

"I'm sure they are fine."

My phone vibrated in my pocket and I pulled it out to see a video call from Emma.

"Speaking of her," Luke muttered.

I answered and saw Emma's glowing smile as she saw us. "Hey you love birds! How's the trip?"

"Very good. I think we're going to stay here forever."

"Send Molly," Luke added.

She laughed. "You guys better come back!"

I rolled my eyes. "We are, don't worry."

Sam appeared beside her with a large grin. "You look homeless with that beard! Chief isn't going to be happy about that, my friend," Sam picked.

"Yeah, yeah," Luke said, scratching his beard that he hadn't shaved all week.

"Is everything going okay with Molly?" I asked, feeling a little concerned about their call.

"Molly is perfect! She's such a good dog, but we actually called to tell you guys something," Emma started, fighting a bigger smile. Sam looked at her and I knew what they were about to tell us before they said it. Emma lifted a black and white sonogram image and said excitedly. "I'm pregnant!"

"Congrats you two!" I said with surprise, even Luke seemed shocked.

"Thanks! We've just hit three months today and we wanted to tell you guys first," Emma explained.

"We're honored," Luke said, sounding genuine, "and excited for you."

We asked the normal questions about how Emma was feeling and when she was due. We got off not long after and Luke and I stared at each other.

"Wow," we both said then laughed.

"That was quick," Luke murmured, letting his arms fall from around me.

"I mean they've been married for several months."

He ran a hand through his hair and blew out a breath. "Emma and Sam are going to be parents. That's just..."

"Crazy?" I laughed.

He chuckled. "I guess it's not. I mean...do we want kids?"

I thought about his question. We hadn't talked about it that much except maybe one day we'd like them but definitely not now.

"Yes, I think so, right?"

He looked at me and I could see him trying to figure it out. "We don't need to make any decisions right now. We just got married, let's enjoy married life." I agreed, touching his arm.

"You're right. No kid talk right now. That's a whole other conversation I think."

Yes...yes it was. And a conversation for a future time but right now, I was going to enjoy the last few hours of my honeymoon with my husband.

Author's Notes

What They Don't Tell You About Divorce was just supposed to be a standalone book, but after going through getting remarried, I realized that Brynn and Luke weren't done sharing their story.

There are only a few scenarios in WTDTYAGR that were mirrored off my own life and the most prominent one was when Brynn thinks Luke is proposing.

It was an ice festival in our town and my husband and I had been dating for a little over a year at that point. Dan kept acting weird and insisted on going on a carriage ride. My mind went racing and I was so nervous because as much as I loved him, I didn't feel ready to get married again.

That night he fidgeted in his pocket several times, and I started sweating like crazy, thinking 'Oh God, this is the night.' When we couldn't do a carriage ride, he seemed disappointed, so he pulled me off to the side and I saw him reaching in his pocket. I felt as if I was going to pass out! When his hand returned with nothing, I was left feeling confused and to my surprise, disappointed. I confronted him when we got home, and he was shocked I thought he was proposing. When I demanded to know what was in his pocket, he explained he had a bug bite that he was trying to scratch inconspicuously.

You can imagine how stupid I felt! But it was at that moment I realized I wanted to get remarried again because of *him*.

It finally happened on our two year anniversary on the beach, and it was just us. I may have asked him multiple times in tears "are you sure?" because I was a basket case and he still wanted to marry me!

The week we got married was a week from hell, just like poor Emma. My husband's best man/best friend disappeared for a few days without contacting anyone, I had a contact stuck in my eye, our pastor had to cancel on us due to being sick, and our DJ was in the hospital. Even though it was a horrible week, Dan and I became even closer through all hardships.

Things did work out and we had a pastor to marry us, the best man showed up, our DJ was able to make it, and the pesky contact did come out of my eye. We said I do in front of our family and friends, and it made the week from hell completely worth it.

This book is for all those divorcees who are in a new relationship either right after your divorce or years later. Don't be afraid to get remarried. If you find your person, it should feel…right, like it was always supposed to be them.

Acknowledgements

It has been a long time coming with publishing WTDTYAGR. There were lots of late nights and early mornings when my baby girl was asleep because I didn't want to miss out on anything in her life. Publishing was put on the back burner so I'm grateful it's done.

Thank you to my mom for always being my editor, hair stylist, babysitter, and nurse. You are my best friend.

A big shout out to one of my best author friends, Emma, who was the first person to edit WTDTYAGR. I appreciate your help and support the last year!

Thank you to Jenny, Lynnea, and Kristin for beta reading and hyping me up while they read. Your encouragement made me smile and feel blessed to have you in my life!

Thank you to my sister-in-law for editing and being my last set of us on the book!

Thank you to my husband for dealing with me as I spent many hours prepping for publishing. Thank you also for coming with me to signings and being support, but couldn't sell a book because he's never read them before (haha!)

And lastly, thank you to all my friends, family, and fans who have supported me through the years. I love hearing how much my books have impacted you.

Especially when several of you shared your own Before Meeting Him Lists! Keep that up!

Other Books by J.K. Weyant

The Dorothea & Browen Trilogy

Dragon's Pick

Dragon's Loss

Dragon's Fall

About the Author

J.K.Weyant is an independent author who has been writing since she was thirteen years old. With encouragement from family, friends, and her husband, she made the jump to self-publish. J.K. Weyant has a love for fantasy and romance novels and a way to travel wherever she wants with just reading words from a book. She hopes she can bring laughter, joy and adventure to all who reads her stories.

If you enjoyed my book, please share with friends and family to get the word out! You can also follow me on Instagram and Facebook for updates on book releases and other news. Or you can join my newsletter chain!

https://www.facebook.comJK-Weyant-104865088842555
https://www.instagram.com/jkweyantauthor82/
jkweyantauthor@gmail.com

www.ingramcontent.com/pod-product-compliance
Lightning Source LLC
LaVergne TN
LVHW020540100826
845148LV00010B/1551

* 9 7 9 8 9 8 6 3 1 0 3 7 4 *